'Oh, Clare, you're killing me.' David's hands moved up stiffly, as if against his will, to cup her shoulders under the loose sleeves of her blouse, thumbs moving over the soft skin as he dragged her down towards him. 'I promised myself I wasn't going to touch you. Why didn't you refuse me?' he demanded thickly.

'I wanted it too,' she admitted breathlessly.

'You shouldn't,' he told her, watching helplessly as his hands moved down to the glossy satin curve of her breasts, tracing the lucky freckles that kissed her creamy skin to their hiding place in her generous cleavage. Her breasts seemed to rise against his fingers, trapping them in their shadowed valley. 'You know what I am, what my life is like. Are you prepared to let me do this in the knowledge of all our differences? Knowing that I can't possibly be comfortably slotted into your secure little world?' His eyes rose to hers, narrowing. 'Or is that precisely *why* you're inviting me to make love to you. Because you *know* I won't be here in a week? Are you just looking for a passing prince to reawaken your sexuality, someone who won't cause complications afterwards?'

A BEWITCHING COMPULSION

BY

SUSAN NAPIER

MILLS & BOON LIMITED
ETON HOUSE   18-24 PARADISE ROAD
RICHMOND   SURREY   TW9 1SR

First published in Great Britain 1989
by Mills & Boon Limited

© Susan Napier 1989

Australian copyright 1989
Philippine copyright 1989
This edition 1989

ISBN 0 263 76500 8

Set in Times Roman 10 on 10½ pt.
01-8912-62743 C

Made and printed in Great Britain

CHAPTER ONE

'I'M very sorry, Mrs Malcolm, but I had no idea that you'd have such strong objections. I thought you'd be *pleased*. After all, it's quite an honour.'

It was difficult to smile when you were shaking with anger, but Clare managed it fairly credibly. The woman was obviously bewildered and upset, and who could blame her? Of course she'd had no idea, the person who *was* to blame had made very sure of that!

'It's all right, Mrs Carmen, what's done is done. But in future I think you might be wise to check with the child's *parents* before undertaking such an ambitious scheme.'

'But I thought I had. I mean, Mrs Malcolm... Mrs Malcolm *senior* said...' The unfortunate woman trailed off, looking from Clare's angry face to the proudly set one of her mother-in-law.

'I can imagine,' Clare clipped grimly, giving Virginia Malcolm a fulminating stare.

'I really am very sorry,' stuttered Mrs Carmen, shifting awkwardly from foot to foot in the shabby gentility of the small room. She was obviously longing to be gone, and Clare's anger suddenly drained away in sympathy. She, too, longed to escape the tensions that Virginia was a genius at creating.

'I know you meant well,' Clare managed another smile, 'and I appreciate the thought behind the action. It's just that I think Tim is a little young for the kind of pressures that performing in public bring.'

'Oh, but he enjoyed it. He wasn't nervous at all. Excited, yes, but not frightened. And a Master Class isn't really a public performance——'

'As I said, I appreciate the thought,' Clare cut her off
firmly. She knew all the arguments—Virginia trotted
them out with aggravating regularity. 'But at the moment
I'm content for him just to have his regular lessons. I
hope he thanked you for the outing...?'

Mrs Carmen allowed herself to be guided to the front
door of the compact townhouse, relief mixing with her
flustered embarrassment over the awkward situation. 'He
did, and very nicely too. He's a lovely little boy, Mrs
Malcolm.'

And I want him to stay that way, the thought drifted
across Clare's mind as her mouth tugged down wryly.
'I only wish his schoolteachers thought the same. If he
paid as much attention to his work as he does to his
music and manners, I'd be charmed myself.' She dredged
up sufficient small-talk to see the woman off pleasantly,
to indicate that she was forgiven, but when she sought
out her mother-in-law a few minutes later she felt anything but forgiving.

Virginia was making tea in the narrow kitchen which
overlooked her small, well-tended garden.

'How could you, Virginia? How could you do such a
thing without asking me first?'

'I knew you'd say no,' Virginia said with a smugness
she must know was irritating. Clare's mouth drew into
a tight line as she stared at her mother-in-law. Virginia
was smartly dressed and made-up, her short hair with
its elegant grey rinse set in a flattering style. She carried
her years well. Anyone looking at her would think that
here was a kind-hearted, contented woman with a very
positive approach to her declining years. In many ways
she *was* exactly what she appeared to be, but there were
other, less attractive forces at work that had caused much
conflict within her family. Her stubborn, 'mother knows
best' attitude towards her son, and her refusal to accept
him for himself, had led to Lee's virtual estrangement
from his parents for several years after his marriage to
Clare. After his father's death from a heart attack the

breach was healed, but after Lee's own death Clare often had cause to regret that Virginia hadn't kept to her original intention of washing her hands entirely of any responsibility for her son or his family. Having been independent herself from the age of sixteen, when her widowed mother had died, Clare found it tough to try to live up to the maternal expectations of someone to whom she had no ties but those of duty.

'And you knew *why* I'd say no. We've been over and over this, Virginia——'

'Well, you must admit you've got a blind spot about this, Clare——'

'*I've* got a blind spot?' Clare was torn between anger and amusement.

'Yes. Just because Lee turned his back on his classical training to take up with that awful band——' His mother shuddered at the memory of the group which Lee had formed and performed with as lead guitarist and vocalist. The fact that Kraken had been a raging success made no difference to her. Virginia was an accomplished pianist with very narrow classical tastes. Any other form of music wasn't worth considering, especially the 'noise' that modern rock bands turned out. '——doesn't mean that you shouldn't give his son a chance to exercise his talent.'

'Tim isn't even seven yet!' Clare was on familiar ground. Virginia's arguments were as narrow as her musical tastes. 'He has two lessons a week and he practises every day. On top of that he has all his normal schoolwork. He's not ready to cope with the kind of things you want to throw at him.'

'If you didn't live in that God-forsaken place Tim could have proper lessons and I wouldn't *have* to go behind your back to give him the opportunities he deserves.'

There it was. The 'mother knows best' argument. Only in this case *Clare* was the mother, and she didn't take her responsibilities lightly.

'Rotorua is hardly a wilderness, Virginia. It's one of New Zealand's foremost tourist centres——'

'Tourists!' Virginia sniffed disparagingly as she arranged the tea-tray and handed it to Clare to carry through to the lounge. 'If you lived here in Auckland you'd have access to the best violin teachers *and* the best facilities. And I could see a bit more of the only family I have left...'

One reason why Clare chose to live two hundred and fifty kilometres away!

'Cheryl Tyson is a very good violinist in her own right, as well as being a very experienced teacher,' she said, setting the tray on the coffee-table, trying to remain patient. They had the rest of the weekend to get through before she and Tim returned to the lodge and she'd rather spend it reasonably amicably. At least Virginia had the decency not to involve Tim directly in their 'discussions', as she called them, about his future. Except for today. Today was unforgivable.

'Tim needs more than just a good teacher, he needs the best. He's not just gifted, Clare, he's *blessed*. He's...he's a wunderkind. He could be another Heifetz! Did you know that Heifetz played the Mendelssohn Concerto when he was only six?'

Of course Clare knew. Virginia never passed up the opportunity to thrust another musical autobiography or book about gifted children on her daughter-in-law. Clare had long ago faced the fact that her son was exceptional, but she was a more critical reader than Virginia— she absorbed the cons as well as the pros of childhood exploitation. Her first consideration must always be Tim's health and happiness, not her own or her mother-in-law's ambitions for him.

'Let's just agree to disagree, shall we? *I'm* Tim's mother, and ultimately *I* make the decisions—about where we live and what sort of education he has. If you can't accept that, I'm sorry, but I won't have you interfering the way you did today. If you do, then I'm afraid Tim and I won't be able to come and stay any more. I won't have my parental authority undermined or disregarded, however strongly you feel you have a valid motive.'

Virginia's face was stiff with offended pride, but she didn't misjudge her daughter-in-law's quietness. It was when she was quiet that Clare was at her most serious. In fact, she was very well-named—there was a cool clarity, a stillness about Clare that misled people into thinking that she was easy to read. But, like a clear pond of water, she had an uncanny knack of reflecting one's own thoughts and feelings without revealing her own. And yet with some people—Tim for one—she possessed a passionate warmth and humour that left the onlooker feeling subtly deprived. It was an aggravating feeling, and one that Virginia had to strive not to resent. Whatever their differences of opinion, there was no arguing that Clare was a conscientious and loving mother.

'I thought that Tim would enjoy seeing Deverenko in action,' she said placatingly.

'I'm sure he did, but that's not the point. Getting tickets to attend a Master Class is one thing, *participating* is quite another,' Clare pointed out drily. 'It must have taken a considerable amount of manoeuvring to achieve...since the students for these things are usually selected weeks in advance, and are supposedly all from the University School of Music.'

Virginia shook her head, 'This was one of a series for all ages and levels that Deverenko has been holding around the country. It was just a matter of auditioning——'

'But Tim didn't audition!'

'I gave Mrs Carmen that tape you sent me...of Tim doing the *Fantasie Pastorale*,' Virginia admittedly uncomfortably, revealing the secret she had been nursing for a month. 'She was really excited at the thought of bringing him to Deverenko's notice, and as she's a violin tutor at the School of Music, her recommendation carries a lot of weight.'

'I see.' Clare made a mental note that in future Virginia would have to keep up with Tim's progress on the violin second-hand, by letter, rather than the tape recordings that Clare had been obligingly posting off every month.

'No, you don't see, Clare. If only you had *been* there!' Virginia conveniently forgot that that had been the last thing she had wanted when she'd made her furtive plans. 'Deverenko was really impressed, with Tim's whole demeanour as well as his playing. You should have seen the way he watched him, the way Tim blossomed under the attention! And he talked with us...Mrs Carmen and I...for quite a long while afterwards. He thinks that he has a place for Tim at his school!'

'I told you, I'm quite satisfied with his progress——'

'But this is something else. He'd be one of the famous David Deverenko's protégés! Think of the doors that would open to Tim. His school is very select—he only has about twenty-five children there—and imagine Tim being taught by one of the world's greatest violinists!'

'I don't suppose that Deverenko does much of the actual teaching,' said Clare dampeningly. 'He has a fairly full concert schedule, performing all over the world. I don't think he's ready to retire into teaching just yet, do you?'

'But he helps shape the programme, and they regularly invite famous musicians to conduct guest classes. Oh, Clare, how could you turn down a chance like this? It might never come again!'

'If Tim is as good as you say he is, it'll come again—in a year or so, when he's better able to handle it. Besides—the Deverenko school is a boarding-school, isn't it? And there's the question of fees——'

'They waive them in special cases—Deverenko told me himself. For that matter, Clare, I'd sell this place if it meant that Tim could have his chance——'

The sobering thing was that she meant it. Any sacrifice was worth launching her grandson on the career that had been denied herself, through family obligations, and her son—through Lee's own curtailing of a promising career as a classical guitarist.

'No, Virginia.'

'At least talk to the man. He's going to get in touch——'

'There's no point, Virginia. Not for another year at least. Now, the subject is closed...' Again the quiet implacability that it was unwise to ignore.

It was a pity that Clare couldn't use the same tactics on her son. When Virginia called Tim down from the small upstairs bedroom that he and Clare shared when they came to stay, he was full of his news.

'Hey, Mummy, guess what I did while you were out shopping?' He looked very pleased with himself as he helped himself to the afternoon tea that had lured him away from his quiet absorption in a book. Tim's concentration was fearful. Whether he was playing his half-sized violin, or reading, or just thinking, he displayed a deafness to distraction which was both the joy and the bane of his teachers' existences—and his mother's. Only food could penetrate his mental shell, although one would never know it from his thinness. Tim had inherited his mother's tallness and pale blonde hair, but not her build. Clare wasn't fat, but her curves could get away from her if she didn't watch herself. Lee *had* been inclined to plumpness, but all he seemed to have bequeathed to his son was his brown eyes, and the lightning flashes of humour that sometimes made them dance with mischief.

'Your granny has just been telling me,' Clare said, watching him devour the biscuits on his plate with ruthless efficiency.

'The maestro said I had an instinct.'

'Did he?' Damn the maestro.

'Yes, he said I could make the violin speak.'

'Did he?'

For Tim's sake she showed an avid interest as he repeated every single thing that the awe-inspiring maestro had said about his playing, both good and bad—there seemed to be a fairly even mix of both, and Clare detected in Tim a faint air of chagrin. Most people were so astounded by his virtuosity in relation to his age that they heaped praise upon him. Perhaps the experience would be of value after all.

'*And* he's going to send us some tickets to his next concert in Auckland. It's next week. Can we go, Mummy? Can we go and see him play? I've heard him on the radio and on tapes, but that's not the same as *seeing* him.'

Clare felt a pang at the sight of the shining adoration on the small face. David Deverenko had certainly made an impression on her son, for better or for worse. Tim was a fairly biddable boy, except where music was concerned. There he was quite fierce, and he was quite capable of making life a misery for a long time to come if she didn't grant this perfectly reasonable request.

'We'll see,' she temporised lamely, and he grinned hugely, showing the gap where a front tooth was coming through. He knew that resigned tone of voice...a little boy with perfect pitch could scarcely miss it. They would go to his concert!

She took him out for a walk in a nearby park during the evening. It was a struggle to get Tim to take any form of exercise—other than with his bowing arm!— but Clare insisted on a certain amount of fresh air and tried to make it palatable for him by making it 'their' time of the day. In her job as receptionist-manager for a secluded hotel on the shores of Lake Rotama she was usually kept busy from dawn to dusk, and making time for her son was very important for both of them.

This evening, however, she curtailed the walk when every conversation worked itself around to the wonderful David Deverenko—how he was ten feet tall and had the face of a god and the voice of an angel and magical powers over everything musical... or that was how Tim's artless description sounded to Clare. She didn't mind Tim having heroes—and ever since he had been old enough to turn on the radio they had been musicians—but a *super*-hero was tough to compete with. Mere mums didn't stand a chance!

Fortunately Virginia knew when to hold her tongue, and didn't add her enthusiasm to Tim's over the dinner-table, or Clare might very well have made a tart observation about the earthly origins of the World's Greatest Living Violinist that would have shattered her credibility for some time to come in her son's hero-dazzled eyes.

Half-way through dessert, the telephone rang. The two women looked at each other across the table. Virginia half rose.

'I'd better get it,' she said reluctantly.

Clare sighed. 'No, I will.' She went out into the kitchen and picked up the phone. When she re-entered the dining-room her face was tight with annoyance.

'Who was it?' asked Virginia cautiously, glancing sideways at Tim's blond head, bent deliriously over his favourite pavlova.

'A newspaper. Wanting a photograph.'

'Oh.'

'Yes, oh.' Clare spoke calmly, so as not to alert Tim. 'Just the thing I wanted to avoid. Someone thought they'd be interested in a "new phenomenon". They even,' she added, voice quivering with annoyance despite her restraint, 'had some kind of comment from a *certain* prominent person in the field.' Her grim tone explicitly indicated who that prominent person was.

Virginia pursed her lips. She couldn't see what Clare's objection was. In her opinion, the more people who knew about Tim's talent, the better. It was almost criminal of Clare to try and hide it away as if it were something to be ashamed of. Wisely, however, she said nothing.

There were two more phone calls before Tim was finally tucked up in bed; it being Saturday night he was allowed to stay up later than usual. The first was from a rival newspaper, the second from a local television regional news reporter. By the time the third call came, Clare was fed up with people who wouldn't take no for an answer.

'Yes, who is this, please?' she demanded in an icy tone as she snatched up the offending instrument.

'Mrs Malcolm?' The voice of an angel. Clare fought the impulse to slam the receiver back down.

'Who is this?'

'David Deverenko. Virginia suggested I call.' *Virginia?* First-name terms already? It had taken Clare four months of 'Mrs Malcolm' and an engagement ring before she had been invited to use 'Virginia'.

'Mrs Malcolm?'

'Yes, I'm here,' said Clare reluctantly, staring at her reflection in the shiny kettle on the bench. Her face looked quite pale and, combined with the thick, wavy, shoulder-length blonde hair and cream kitchen walls behind her, looked rather ghostly. She blinked. There was no room for ghosts in her life, real or imagined.

'It's about your son, Timothy. Did Virginia mention that I wanted to talk to you about his future?'

'His present, don't you mean?'

There was a slightly startled silence. 'If you mean the possibility of his studying at my school here, yes. That's where I'm ringing from, in fact. I know you're leaving the city tomorrow evening, but I thought that perhaps we could have some initial discussion——'

'I'm afraid that's not possible,' Clare cut in hastily, having drifted slightly in her fascination with that rich, dark, musical voice. He wasn't mesmerising *her* with his song! 'Virginia seems to have misled you——'

'You already have Tim accepted somewhere else?' The mellow voice sharpened critically.

'No, I——'

'I thought not. There *is* no other equivalent facility to the Deverenko School—not in this country, anyway. Are you considering taking him overseas?'

'No, I——'

'Good. I can save you the trouble. My school can provide Timothy with a very well-balanced musical education. Anything less for a boy who shows his promise would be unthinkable.'

Oh, it would, would it? Another narrow-minded musician trying to tell her that music was the only choice for her son.

'*If* you would let me finish at least *one* of my sentences——' Clare said tartly, and there was the sound of a faintly indrawn breath, followed by a silence that seemed anything but meek. 'Thank you. As I was saying, Virginia seems to have misled you. She did not have my permission to allow Tim to take part in your Master Class, and I have no interest in placing him in your school.'

'No interest? Mrs Malcolm, you don't seem to understand——'

'No, *you* don't understand, Mr Deverenko.' Clare was tired and cross, or she would never have been so rude. Being a parent toughened one to standing up to outside threat, but Clare hated confrontations. She had a shy person's fear of drawing attention to herself. But in this mood, protected by the anonymity of the telephone, she overcame her shyness. 'I didn't solicit your help and I don't require it. And neither do I appreciate your speaking to the Press about my son.'

'I only——'

'I don't want to hear your excuses, Mr Deverenko. I refuse to be hounded by you *or* your friends in the Press.'

She could feel herself blushing furiously as she hung up the phone, cutting across his explosive protest, and the reflection in the kettle confirmed it. She pressed a cool hand against her hot cheek. Even though no one had witnessed her behaviour, she felt embarrassed. She had been very rude and probably unfair, given the fact that he had been as much a victim as she and Mrs Carmen, but she had sensed that being offensively brusque was the only way to get rid of a man like David Deverenko. Although he had been born in New Zealand, both his parents were Russian and, from all reports, he had a thoroughly Russian temper—and the pride to match. He had certainly sounded arrogant, even when he was being polite, and musicians of his stature were notoriously single-minded. She only hoped she had succeeded in thoroughly putting him off. After his New Zealand concert he was off to a series of engagements in London, so she doubted he would have the time to spare to pursue a reluctant pupil. Perhaps now he wouldn't send the tickets to his concert, either—Clare knew that it had been booked out the week that the box-office opened—thereby freeing her of the obligation to take Tim. Tim would be disappointed, but better a temporary disappointment than a prolonged, serious division of his loyalties. Clare had no intention of playing the villainess to Deverenko's hero, which would be the role assigned to her if she allowed him any quarter.

After giving Virginia a brief, edited version of the content of the call, Clare went up to bed herself, although it was a long time before she could force herself to sleep. At times like this she missed her husband badly. His confidence in her as a woman, a wife and mother had bolstered her own. He had respected her opinions even when he'd disagreed with them, and had never tried to ride roughshod over them the way his mother was attempting to do. Lee had never been underhand, always open and direct. He had been full of fun and laughter, and even two years after his death Clare still found herself thinking, 'I must tell Lee about that one,' when she saw or heard of an amusing incident that would have appealed to his offbeat sense of humour.

Sunday lunch was something of an occasion at Virginia's. Lee had been an only child, but Virginia had two sisters and two brothers-in-law, and Sunday was considered family 'visiting day'. In honour of Clare and Tim's visit the lunch was being held at Virginia's, although it was quite a squash with the additional wives and husbands and children. To Clare's relief Tim mixed well with the other children—he was inclined to be impatient and dismissive of those of his peers who didn't share his interests, and resented social encroachments on his love of solitary pursuits. However, most of his cousins were several years older than him and had obviously been well-coached to 'make allowances'. The afternoon went so well that Tim cheerfully went off on a visit to the Auckland Museum with one of his lesser known relations.

'Kim only plays the recorder, but she's OK,' Tim allowed magnanimously as Clare hid a grin, 'for a girl, that is.'

A dozen children and their assorted toys had wreaked a small amount of havoc on Virginia's neat yard, and one of the last guests to leave helped Clare tidy up. Ray had been the closest of Lee's cousins, and a fringe member of Kraken before the band had begun making a name for itself and adopted a thoroughly professional approach. For that reason, and the fact that he rode a motorcycle and wore the leathers to match, he and Virginia didn't get on particularly well, but Clare enjoyed his friendship. In many ways he reminded her of her husband, especially in his laid-back optimism and the wickedly teasing grin he often wore.

As they worked, she told Ray about the events of the previous day and he gave her his full support.

'Aunt Virginia means well, but often they're the worst kind...give her an inch and she'll take a mile. Or should that be millimetres and kilometres? Just shrug it off with a laugh, Clare, that's the only way to deal with her...if you take her seriously, you're done for. What you need, my good woman, is a good man to stand shoulder to shoulder with. Any candidates on the horizon?'

'It's only been two years, Ray.' Lee's death, from a form of leukaemia, had been frighteningly swift, with no remissions.

'A long time to be alone.'

'I've had Tim.' Ray gave her a challenging look. 'I just haven't met anyone who's come close to making me feel ... *anything*.'

'What about all those disgustingly rich guests who tuck themselves away in your retreat? They can't all be blind.'

'Oh, I get plenty of *passes*, Ray,' she laughed at him. 'I'm just being choosy.'

'Lee's a hard act to follow; the guy'll have his work cut out. Of course, you *could* keep it all in the family...' He leered suggestively at her.

'For that, Ray Cowling, you can climb up that plum tree and fetch down that kite.' A makeshift newspaper and bamboo version was enmeshed in the topmost branches.

Ray followed her glance. 'The branches up there are too thin, they'd never hold my weight.' Ray was a solidly built young man, and Clare was inclined to agree. 'What we need here is a slender blonde sylph.'

'I'm hardly sylphlike,' said Clare drily, 'and I'm too old to be climbing trees.'

'Twenty-seven isn't old. Why, you're not even ripe yet ... you won't hit your stride till you're thirty. Come on, I'll give you a leg-up. Hang on, let me take my jacket off first.'

Ray carefully took off his black leather pride and joy, revealing a fashionably ragged black T-shirt that showed off the bulging muscles in his arms. He struck a pose and Clare giggled.

'Promise you won't look up my dress?'

'Nope.' He panted realistically and she laughed again, looking nothing like the cool, shy person that she was when she was uncomfortable or unsure. 'Tuck it between your legs. As a dancer, you should be used to flinging yourself about in next to nothing.'

'A leotard is a great deal more circumspect than lace panties,' said Clare primly, but she tucked up her skirt as he had suggested and he hoisted her up into the spreading branches.

'Ouch!' The twigs were spiky, and as she negotiated them showers of dried leaves were shaken down on to Ray's upturned face.

'Great legs, Clare!'

'Shut up!' Although she had grown too tall for classical ballet, Clare still enjoyed going to jazz ballet and 'jazzercise' classes for fun, and even filled in for the instructor now and then at the gym she attended in Rotorua. Lee had always told her that she had the legs of a chorus girl.

She retrieved the crumpled kite and tossed the remains, with its tangled ball of string, to the ground. Going down was not quite as simple as going up, and Ray's ridiculous teasing didn't help.

'Look, Ray, will you be quiet? I can't laugh and climb at the same time.'

'Doesn't say much for your co-ordination, old girl. Why don't you jump from there? I'll catch you.'

'I bet you will,' said Clare, not trusting him an inch.

'Cross my heart. Would I risk letting you damage one of those glamorous legs?'

Clare didn't really mean to jump, but the flexible soles of her canvas espadrilles slipped suddenly, and to save herself from a thicket of branches she flung herself downwards. Ray caught her, but he was off balance and she wrapped her arms and legs frantically around him as he staggered backwards and fell against the rough tree-trunk, banging his head hard enough to make his eyes water.

'Oh, Ray, I'm sorry. Are you all right?'

He blinked manfully. 'I'm enjoying every minute of it. It's not often I get women crawling all over me. Shall we do it right here like this, or should we take our clothes off first?'

'*Ray!*'

Clare's laughter-choked protest was echoed by a horrified one from several yards behind them. With an
inward groan Clare detached herself from the wickedly
amused Ray to turn and explain to her mother-in-law.
She was rooted to the spot when she discovered that
Virginia was not alone.

Beside her stood a tall, dark man in a black polo-neck
sweater and jeans, staring at Clare with a mixture of
disapproval and bold sexual appraisal. Clare stiffened,
instinctively pressing her splayed hands protectively
across her bared upper thighs, which the bold black eyes
seemed to find of particular interest. Her silent groan
became a moan as she had no difficulty in identifying
the famous face.

David Deverenko had come to call.

CHAPTER TWO

CLARE'S hands were trembling with embarrassment as she untucked her skirt and smoothed it back down around her knees, even though she knew it wasn't going to redeem the wanton image she had just presented. Damn Virginia for springing this on her! She could at least have had the decency to come out and warn Clare that he was here.

She hardly heard Virginia's reproving questions or Ray's rumbling amusement as he explained the circumstances of their clinch, she was far too conscious of the silent penetration of the dark eyes which watched her fumble with her clothing. He wasn't even trying to make the pretence of polite disinterest, and the faint tilt at one corner of his mouth made a mockery of Ray's explanation. How dared he insult her with his disbelief?

She wasn't going to allow herself to be flustered any longer. Let him think what he liked. She raised her eyebrows and stared back at him coolly, eyes grey with disdain. The only defence for shyness was directness; staring someone in the eye always projected an impression of confidence...or so it had proved in the past. Unfortunately, looking at David Deverenko, her eyes had a tendency to wander.

He was not as tall as she had first thought, under six foot, in fact, but the squarish shoulders and compact muscularity of his body beneath the close-fitting clothes exuded command—over himself and others. His skin was olive, and broad Slavonic cheekbones and a hawkish nose bore aggressive testament to his Russian ancestry. Not handsome, Clare decided, then her eyes met his again and she was not so sure. His eyes were very aware, holding a brooding intelligence that refined the harshness of his features.

'Your mother's expecting you back for tea, isn't she, Ray?' Virginia was saying pointedly. 'I'll see you off on that dreadful machine of yours while Mr Deverenko talks to Clare. Take him into the lounge, Clare, and I'll bring a tray through when it's ready.'

Ray gave Clare a resigned grin and, with a quick glance at the silently waiting visitor, leaned over to give her an unnecessarily warm goodbye kiss, taking the opportunity to whisper teasingly, 'Chin up, Goldilocks, the Russian bear won't eat you. He lives on porridge, remember. Odds on he'd never catch you!'

For once his humour didn't register. Clare watched them go down the garden path towards the side gate in the high fence before turning towards the house and saying stiffly, 'If you'd like to come this way, Mr Deverenko...'

David Deverenko followed her thoughtfully, his faint amusement at the entertaining scene fading. He wouldn't have been human if he hadn't, after her rudeness the previous night, rather enjoyed her discomfort, but he was aware it could work against him. Her continued antagonism would make his self-appointed championship of her son that much more difficult.

How to handle it? The problem was that Virginia Malcolm had given him a very sketchy, incomplete picture of Timothy's mother. He had expected someone cool and self-contained, a very reserved woman with a host of emotional anxieties stemming from her husband's death, anxieties that she was projecting on to her son. The artist in David had revolted at the thought of great musical talent being stifled by the clinging of a neurotic woman. She had certainly been 'clinging' a few minutes ago, but not in the context that he had expected.

Pondering the best approach, David's eyes fell to the trim ankles in front of him and he idly shortened his stride, dropping back in order to get another look at her legs. Her calves were slender and beautifully shaped, and the fine interplay of muscles as she walked indicated femininity modified by strength. In spite of the tense set of her spine, she moved with a natural grace enhanced by the subtle refinements of teaching. He wondered whether the thick tangle of her hair was naturally the colour of pale honey, and then, remembering her startlingly pale skin with its liberal sprinkling of freckles, decided that it was. That very fair complexion would burn easily, which was probably why, unlike most New Zealand women at the end of a long, spectacular summer, she didn't have a tan.

Clare excused herself for a few minutes when they reached the lounge, he presumed to have a few trenchant words with her mother-in-law, but when she came back David's amusement was revived. She had used the time to arm her defences. Her hair was returned to sleekness and her blouse had been firmly tucked back into her skirt and buttoned to the hilt. She had used powder, too, to disguise the freckles on her face, as if they might weaken her authority, and her demeanour was brisk and businesslike. She looked him dead in the eye as she invited him to be seated, and he was careful not to show his amusement at her tactics. What was it, he wondered, that rendered those cool grey eyes under their unfashionably thick and straight brows so ineffective? Her mouth, he decided. It was rather small for her face, but sweetly full. A perfect bow. However cold and stern her manner, that mouth would always give her away. Confident now, David relaxed. Her concern with her appearance revealed her vulnerability. All he had to do was to show her that his was the superior strength and authority, and she would be ripe for persuasion. The insecure—male and female—usually responded to the disconcerting mixture of aggression and charm that came naturally to him. Face to face, Clare Malcolm didn't have a chance... and her son would be able to have his...

'Well, Mr Deverenko. Why did you want to talk to me?' Clare sat down opposite him, her hands folded in her lap, her shoulders squared.

In contrast, David Deverenko lounged. Admittedly he did it very well. 'Games, Mrs Malcolm? You may have time for them, but I don't. You know very well why I'm here to see you. Your son Timothy.'

His loaded patience was designed to make her feel silly for her pretence of ignorance. Awed, too, by the great man's condescension, no doubt.

'Really? You surprise me. I thought I made my opinion quite clear on the subject last night.'

'Opinions can change.'

'Not mine.'

'Are you so inflexible, then? That must make the task of bringing up a young child on your own doubly difficult.'

He had her there. Parenting was nothing if not the knack of constantly adjusting oneself to new crises. Children were adept at finding loopholes in hard and fast rules, particularly bright children like Tim. Clare smiled unwillingly at one particularly vivid memory, then hurriedly smoothed it out as she saw David Deverenko staring at her left cheek. Her hand automatically went up to brush away the dimple that gave her smile its funny lopsidedness. As a child her Shirley Temple cuteness had many times enabled her to escape the consequences of mischief, but who took an adult with a baby-dimple seriously?

'Mr Deverenko,' she said severely, to counteract the dimple's effect, 'I——'

'David—please call me David. We can't have a proper argument unless we're on insultingly easy terms.'

'*Mr* Deverenko——'

'I stand corrected,' he murmured ruefully, and at her frigid look put a finger to his lips. His hands were the only thing about him that looked refined—strong, yet with a delicate flexibility that indicated their sensitivity, their skill.

'I don't intend to argue with you. Tim is too young for the kind of intensive musical training that you have in mind for him...'

'Since you wouldn't listen to me, you don't have any idea what I have in mind for him.'

'Virginia——'

'With respect, nor does your mother-in-law. Mrs Malcolm, I am not an evil Fagin come to steal your child away from your loving arms and turn him into a freak. I'm here to *ask*...to find out what *your* plans for the boy are, and to offer you my advice.'

'Your unbiased advice?'

He hid his satisfaction at this indication that she might consider it. 'Yes.'

'Your *opinion*?'

'Yes.'

'An opinion which, of course, is open to my influence.'

He hesitated, conscious of the trap his arrogance had led him into. He was capable of colouring the truth with emotion and enthusiasm, but the cold lie was beyond him.

'Because if it wasn't...if you had come here with one fixed idea—to persuade me that *my* opinion is without worth—why, then, you'd be guilty of inflexibility, wouldn't you, Mr Deverenko? Which, according to you, is a crime.'

He was no longer lounging. He sat forward, muscular thighs splayed, his elbows resting on his knees, fingers interlocking as his fierce jaw tightened. Clare felt a sense of achievement at the banishment of his former supreme self-confidence.

'I am not without honour in my field——' he began slowly.

'Come now, maestro, let's not be absurdly modest. Please feel free to intimidate me with your undoubted greatness.'

'Dammit, woman!' The bearish growl burst out before he could control himself. He got to his feet, took two stiff strides away, then whirled around, eyes narrowing on her bland expression. 'You're enjoying this, aren't you?' he accused.

'Did you expect me not to? Did you think I'd bow and scrape and accept your sacred word as gospel? Didn't Virginia warn you, Mr Deverenko?'

'Yes, but I didn't believe that anyone could be that blind or that stupid!' He made an expressive sound in a rush of air and looked away from her, uttering what had to be a curse in a language other than English. 'I apologise, Mrs Malcolm,' he said with such stiff revulsion that she knew he was unaccustomed to begging for anything. 'I suppose I've completely blown any chance of getting you to listen to me now. But believe me, I came here out of the best of motives. Arrogant and opinionated as you might think I am, I came here for *Timothy's* sake, not to exercise my ego.'

He looked at her then, and Clare felt the full impact of the black eyes at close quarters. She became aware of the power inside him, the controlled vitality, the musician's unique ability to communicate without words. Tim had that ability. Clare didn't. She had no musical ability whatsoever.

'Do you play an instrument?' he asked suddenly, and she had the unsettling feeling that he had read her mind.

'No,' she said proudly, refusing to apologise for it.

'But you've studied ballet.'

'Why, yes...did Virginia tell you?' She wondered uneasily just what Virginia *had* told him.

He shook his head. 'It's in the way you move. You move to music...you compose with your walk.'

Clare could feel her skin heating, the simplicity of his statement attesting to its sincerity. It was a musician's compliment. 'I always wanted to be a ballerina, but I got too tall and...'

'Shapely?' he murmured helpfully, a glimmer of humour easing his dark expression. 'But you are in very good shape. You still dance?'

'For exercise.'

'And enjoyment?'

She allowed herself a smile, forgetting the effect of the dimple. 'That, too.'

'Then you know how music can move the emotions, can demand the best from us. Clare—Mrs Malcolm——'

'Clare.'

'Clare.' Not a flicker of smugness that he had finally got his own way. 'Music is my life. I have been playing the violin since I was very young, and it has given me more pleasure, more success, demanded more of me than I ever dreamed of in my childish fantasies. I knew that what I had was special, and I knew that there was some inner compulsion in me to play that would direct my life rather than accept any lesser compromise. Natural ability with a musical instrument can be a trap. It's very easy to drift, to "cheat", if you like, when you're so much better than anyone else your age. Many children who are called "gifted" musically when they are small children don't fulfil the promise in later years. It is discipline that makes a true musician, as much as talent and instinct... the day to day grind of practice. I was pushed relentlessly by my parents as a child, and although there were times when I resented it quite fiercely, I can attribute the musician I am today to their care and attention. The early years are so important in forming the habits that sustain one through a lifetime of playing, particularly on the violin, which involves specific muscular co-ordination and development. Genius may be born, but its development to its fullest potential is slow and gradual... otherwise we'd all be burnt out by the time we're twenty.'

'You see it strictly from a musician's point of view,' Clare said quietly. 'You're not telling me anything I don't already know. But Tim isn't just a musically gifted child, he's also a six-year-old boy who's interested in mathematics and science. I want him to grow up as a whole person, not an incomplete one, obsessed with just one aspect of himself. There are some educationalists who think that a child shouldn't be expected to specialise until he's in his teens——'

'Ordinarily, yes ... for the average child, but Timothy is *not* average. He has music inside him that needs to be given form and expression. He told me that he's been playing the violin since he was four...'

'Yes. Lee—my husband—gave him a quarter-sized one for his birthday after he'd been fascinated by a busker in the street. It was a kind of a joke...'

'But he's having lessons—obviously you yourself feel that there is a seriousness about him that demands respect rather than mere humouring. Perhaps you are even a little afraid of it, no?' It was the first indication that his thoughts might not be formulated entirely in English. Clare remembered reading somewhere that until he'd gone to school Russian had been his language. Then had come the visits to America and Europe in search of a teacher for the young Deverenko, culminating in his early acceptance at Juilliard. He now spoke five or six languages fluently.

'Afraid, no. Wary, yes. Just because I don't fully understand his gift it doesn't mean I don't fully appreciate it. Tim *will* have his chance, but not yet. He and his father were very close, and he was severely affected by Lee's death. He withdrew into himself and even now is slow to trust himself to others. I don't think he needs any extra pressures right now.'

'But nor should he be left in isolation——'

Clare stiffened. 'Not everyone has your resources, David. I took this job at the lodge because I needed to work and also be close at hand for Tim.' And she hadn't wanted to take up Virginia's offer to 'help', knowing the tussles of will that her assistance would involve.

'I wasn't necessarily meaning geographical isolation, Clare,' David was quick to reassure her, reassured himself by her automatic use of his Christian name. 'I meant from the company of like-minded children.'

'Tim has enough friends——'

'Ones who share his deep interest in music? With whom he can play and interact without being made to feel self-conscious and "different"? Are you sure you're aware of his *changing* needs? I'm sure that the teacher he's with is very competent, but already I can see flaws in Tim's technique which, if not corrected *now*, will dog his playing for the rest of his life. For example, does he practise on his own, or does his teacher supervise his practice?'

'Naturally Miss Tyson can't give him time every day——'

'Quite. Of course she can't. Tim is no doubt the best of her pupils, but the others still deserve the attention that their parents are paying for. One person can only do so much. At the music school the numbers are small. *All* the children have revealed a natural musical ability. We have many teachers, and the children receive individual lessons as well as lessons in ensemble playing, and their daily practice is supervised so that they're not just perfecting their faults. As to Timothy's personal insecurities—as I said, our numbers are small and the atmosphere is very much a family one. I don't think Timothy would find it at all frightening or intimidating. In fact, he seemed to me a very assured individual.'

'About his music, he is. But I don't want him to feel that he is valued only for his musical talent.'

'Ah.' The dark eyes were enlightened. The absent pacing stopped and he came to sit down opposite her again. 'You have been reading psychology of child development, about gifted children, no?'

'I like to be informed. I don't like to rush into things.'

'I don't think there's any danger of that.' He gave her a smile that revealed the charm which had been almost swamped by his emotional intensity. Clare wondered whether he was as intense about everything he did, or whether it was just music that evoked this enthusiasm. 'And I applaud your caution. But there is a point at which caution may become mere stubbornness. Do not discount what I have said merely because you don't like what I have to say. My school does not produce one-dimensional human beings. Music is only a *part* of the syllabus, although it is naturally a large part. We meet Educational Department standards in all our subjects. Our children range in age from eight to fifteen, and, although we've only been running for ten years, many of our graduates so far have found successful careers in varying fields of music.'

'In a sense, though, it's still rather in the nature of an educational experiment. I mean, how many children have gone the full stretch with you? Surely most of them are admitted at intermediate school level?'

'I wouldn't call it an experiment. I'm not using these children as guinea pigs. We've had withdrawals, but not because of any complaints about our standards or our results—merely children who no longer respond to the musical curriculum.' Antagonism crackled in the air again. David Deverenko didn't take too kindly to any hint of criticism, Clare realised.

'And why eight years old? Why not admit children from the age of five?'

'Because they're not capable of——' He stopped on hearing his own words.

'Quite. I don't see any harm in allowing Tim another year of just being an ordinary boy.'

He was on his feet again. 'You haven't been listening to a word I've been saying, have you?'

Clare rose, too, glad that he was not taller than she. 'Yes, I have, and I see the validity of your arguments. It's *you* who won't see the validity of mine. You don't know Timothy, you don't know me. I thank you for your advice and I'll consider it——'

'But you'll do nothing about it. Don't offer me such an insult to my intelligence. Why don't you just say what you mean? You have no intention of taking my advice.'

'Don't put words into my mouth.'

'Why not? They seem to be more truthful than the mealy-mouthed prevarications *you* put there. Perhaps you are jealous of your son, and this is why you deny him the chance of fulfilment. Because your expectations for an artistic career remain unfulfilled, so must his.'

'How dare you? Who do you think you are?'

'David Deverenko. I am somebody, Clare Malcolm, I have made this of myself. I am allowed to be as I am. I was not held back by an anxious mama, I was not made to pay for her...inadequacies. She was a musician—not of great talent—but she valued mine because it was *of* me, *in* me, indivisible from what I am. Ach!' He threw up the strong, slender, square-tipped hands. 'I have the tenses wrong, but the sentiment, the sentiment you cannot mistake. You have no heart, Clare Malcolm, if you can deny the boy his rightful inheritance. What would your husband have wanted for him? The best? Or the mediocrity of "wait and see"? How dare *you*? And who are *you* to decide?'

'I'm somebody, too,' she threw at him fiercely, her nose shiny from the perspiration of her small temper, her hands clammy with the enormity of what she was doing—offending a man who had every right to believe that his advice would be treated with the utmost respect. But she *couldn't* let him overwhelm her with his force of will and personality; she owed it to Tim to fight for what she believed was right, even though it might cost her an agony of embarrassment in the process. 'I may not be famous, or a wild success at a brilliant career, but I am something that you can never aspire to be, Mr Deverenko—a mother. I have bonds with Tim that you can't possibly understand. I bore him in my body and I know him as intimately as it's possible to know another human being. He knows that I shall love him whatever he is—or isn't—and right now what he needs most is the undemanding reassurance of that love. People like you, Mr Deverenko, so eager to get their hands on him, would crush him with unreasonable expectations. Tim is gifted in other ways, too, but you would ignore that in favour of *your* bias, music. You didn't come here to *ask*, you came here to *tell*. Well, now you've told me, I'd like you to go.'

'Clare——' The fiery Russian temper was reined back sharply as her criticisms stung.

Clare walked to the door and held it open, just as Virginia came through with her best china laid on a tray.

'Oh, were you coming to get me? Are you ready for your tea?'

'Mr Deverenko is just leaving.'

'But...surely you can't have finished?' Virginia looked from one to the other, her heart sinking at Clare's paleness and the violinist's glower.

'Mr Deverenko's time is too valuable to allow him to fritter it away on anxious mamas,' said Clare coldly.

'I don't——'

'Besides, he would never *dream* of outstaying his welcome.' She opened the outer door and stood, ignoring Virginia's fluttering, her wintry expression a silent challenge to his pride. David Deverenko *grovel* for an audience? Never!

David stormed across the footpath to his car, a sleek grey Jaguar parked at the kerb. He slammed his hands against the roof and swore. He stood there a moment, stiff with outrage, then he swore again, more softly, and began to laugh. So much for his aggressive charm! She had routed him far more completely than his fiercest teacher! They had both lost their tempers, but it was she who had triumphed with her damned Cupid's mouth and dimples! How Efrem would laugh. Laugh? He would want to *hire* her. Anyone who could finesse David Deverenko out of the door when he didn't want to go was worth having on the payroll! His fingers tapped impatiently on the sunwarmed car roof. Dammit, since when did he give up so easily?

Clare was still leaning against the closed door, her legs weak with reaction. She had done it. She had actually outfaced the man...stood up for herself! Pride was mixed with the faintly nauseous feeling that always rushed over her after a row.

'You're a fool, Clare,' Virginia told her angrily, the teacups on the tray rattling their disapproval. 'How could you insult him like that? Jeopardise Tim's whole *future*? The day might come when you *need* that man's help——'

'He's not the only violinist in the world.'

'But he's the only one with such strong links with New Zealand. He's committed to helping young New Zealand musicians. Music is a very enclosed little world, you know. A recommendation from him or his school would be more than a foot in the door; it would be the best seat in the house!'

'Well, if he's so committed, he won't turn his back on promise just because of a personal difference of opinion.'

'Difference of opinion? Clare, you were downright hostile!'

'You didn't hear what he said to *me*,' began Clare defensively, niggled by guilt...another unwelcome regular which attended her rows. She hated hurting or upsetting people, even when it was necessary. Her own sensitivity was a definite handicap.

Her confidence was interrupted by a series of sharp raps that vibrated her head against the wooden door. The two women stared at each other for a frozen moment, and then Virginia jerked her head commandingly.

Clare swallowed. She knew very well who was on the other end of those demanding blows, and she didn't know if she had the strength to go through it all again. Reluctantly she opened the door, tempted to use the security chain but for Virginia's hovering presence. Sure enough, David Deverenko stood on the doorstep.

'I forgot to give you these,' he said, holding out an envelope. Clare stared at it mistrustfully, and his dark, musical voice acquired a silky provocation. 'The tickets for my concert. Three of them. I promised Timothy... and I never go back on my word.'

Virginia reached past Clare, the tray hurriedly discarded on the hall table, to take the proffered envelope. 'Oh, thank you, David, we do so appreciate it.' She gave Clare a sharp nudge.

'Yes, thank you,' she said slowly, unwillingly.

'My pleasure, Clare,' he replied smoothly. 'I know you'd hate to disappoint Tim. There's a small supper after the performance which you might like to bring him to as well.' And before she could open her mouth he switched his attention to Virginia. 'I'm sure you'd enjoy meeting some of the orchestra members and patrons. You might like to become a patron yourself, Virginia. The Symphony is always on the lookout for sympathetic support, artistic as well as financial.'

Virginia's eyes lit up, and she flushed under his warm regard. 'I'll look forward to it,' she said breathlessly. 'I'm so glad you're doing the Bruch Concerto—it's one of my favourites. I have you on record, as a matter of fact, and Tim listens to it endlessly...'

Clare could have kicked them both. They were acting as if she weren't even there, as if the last half-hour hadn't happened. All that nervous energy expended for *nothing*.

'Goodbye, Mr Deverenko,' she said pointedly. The last thing she wanted was for Tim to come home and find his hero on the doorstep; he would *never* let him go. He was going to have a blue fit as it was, to hear that the maestro had visited while he was out.

The Russian gave her a smoky smile. '*Au revoir*, Clare,' he said in a voice that vibrated along her spine. Then, satisfied that he had had the last word, he turned and sprang jauntily down the steps, whistling something hauntingly familiar. The Jaguar gave a bearish kind of growl as it drew away from the kerb and Clare watched it go, full of misgivings. What other promises was he prepared to give, and honour, to her son?

Virginia was all for Clare and Tim staying on another week until the concert, but Clare insisted on returning to Rotorua as planned. Tim's problems had meant he had missed quite a bit of schooling the previous year, and although he had quickly made up the academic gap, and indeed leapt ahead in some areas, she thought it important that his routine not be interrupted. She also thought that she had presumed enough on her friendship with Miles Parrish, owner of the Moonlight Lodge. Although, with the fishing season coming to a close, the lodge was only lightly booked for the next few weeks and undergoing renovations, there was always plenty for Clare to do. Miles's interests were many and varied, and even when he was in residence he trusted Clare with most of the responsibility for the smooth running of the lodge which, given its exclusive and wealthy clientele, used to the best of everything, was quite a task. Clare had had no formal training in hotel management, and had made some rather horrendous mistakes early on, but she was a quick learner and knew she owed Miles a great deal for allowing her the luxury of on-the-job training. The pay was good and the tips generous, and she and Tim received full board, so she had been able to save a comfortable amount in the past eighteen months. She and Lee had thought their happiness would last forever, and they hadn't seriously planned for the future. There had been no money when he'd died, and she'd known that Virginia's straitened circumstances had prevented her from offering anything but a roof over their heads and a free child-minding service while Clare had sought a secretarial job. Miles's offer, six months after Lee's death, had been a godsend. It had been a bit of a wrench to leave Auckland, where she had been born and brought up, but she had no family of her own there now and had been conscious of the need to forge a new life for herself and Tim. She had never regretted it.

As it happened, Miles was away for the week, fishing in Florida with an American millionaire who shared his passion for salt-water fly-fishing. Miles had the spirit of an entrepreneur, and the money to indulge it. He intended making a series of videos on fishing around the world, and had persuaded his American friend to invest in it. As a consequence Clare had little time to brood about the concert she was constrained to attend, since the builder and the architect got into a battle royal about a flaw in the design of the extensions to the main lodge, and it was up to her to smooth things over, suggest a compromise and try and keep the two men from carrying their argument over to other aspects of the renovations. There was also the problem of a guest losing a valuable piece of jewellery, a generator failure that caused a meltdown in the freezer during a power-cut, a resignation, a minor flood in one of the guest cottages, and the death, from mysterious injuries, of one of Miles's favourite hunting dogs.

Clare had planned to drive up to Auckland on the morning of the concert but, having been up the previous two nights—first nursing the dog, Chef, then helping stem the flood—Saturday got off to a very shaky start and it was afternoon before she and Tim set off in the lodge stationwagon which Miles had insisted she use whenever she needed it. It didn't help Clare to feel the ominous signs of a cold coming on, and the effort of concentration the four-hour drive took made her feel decidedly woolly by the time they turned into Virginia's driveway. It seemed to her tired brain that Tim had talked non-stop the whole trip, and come time for the concert he was still fresh and eager, whereas Clare felt like a limp piece of string.

The woolliness in her head seemed also to have affected her ears for, sitting in their privileged seats in the stalls and trying, for Tim's benefit, to look as rapt as he thought the situation warranted, Clare seemed to be hearing everything through a lead filter. Her eyes, too, felt like lead, and she surreptitiously rested them every now and then, only afterwards admitting to herself that she might have fallen into a light doze or two. The concert, judging from the standing ovation that prompted two short, wittily introduced encores from the soloist, was a raging success, but Clare was hard put to it to remember anything about it, or the lavish supper that followed. She knew she talked to Deverenko and went through all the motions of eating and drinking and talking to innumerable strangers, but her brain had definitely been on hold. Fortunately nobody seemed to notice anything odd about her zombie-like politeness, and Virginia and Tim were too busy enjoying basking in Deverenko's reflected glory to remark on her listlessness. Clare did recall Deverenko giving her an odd look or two during their unremembered conversation, but then his manner had also been overly polite. Perhaps—horrors—he had noticed her dozing while he had thrown his soul into what the next day's papers had called 'a brilliant, extrovert performance containing both passion and tenderness'. Perhaps her restless shifting of her aching bones in the semi-comfortable seat had impinged on his formidable concentration. Perhaps he now regarded her as more of an ignorant philistine than ever!

One thing she did remember about their conversation—it hadn't touched on the reason for their clash the previous week. Her relief had been mixed with a faint contempt. Oh, he was kind enough to Tim—signing his programme and talking to him about the performance—but obviously his flare of interest had faded and he felt no need to make excuses for it. Well, that suited Clare just fine. He had barged into their lives, he could barge right back out again. The tickets were obviously just a sop to his conscience. One day, when Tim was a famous violinist, Clare would be able to throw it in his face: *this* is what you walked away from! Oh, heavens, what was she thinking? She *must* be sick!

She was. Their stay in Auckland was extended another four days as Clare succumbed to a very bad bout of flu. On the fifth day Miles flew in on a direct flight from Dallas and took them back down to Moonlight in his new toy, a French-built Aerospatial Dauphin helicopter, which he flew himself.

David Deverenko left New Zealand for London on the same day.

CHAPTER THREE

'TIM, are you still in here? It's such a lovely day, why don't you go outside and play for a while? You could take the dogs for a walk.'

'I'm reading.' Tim didn't lift his eyes from his book. He was sprawled on the big, overstuffed couch in the empty lounge of the lodge, a book propped against the arm.

'I would think that after a week of rain you'd be happy to get out in the sunshine for a while,' said Clare in exasperation. 'Why don't you go down to the lake and see if the boat's come in?'

The arrival of autumn had increased Moonlight's isolation. The single, narrow gravelled access road through the bush frequently became impassable after rain, which meant the only way in or out of the small bay on the far side of Lake Romata was by boat...or helicopter. The trip from the main road was usually quicker by water, anyway, but the road was a winding, scenic route that made up for in beauty what it lacked in convenience.

'We would have heard the motor, if it had,' said Tim, with the aggravating logic that grated on so many of his teachers. If they weren't accusing him of being inattentive, they were finding that his full attention could be even more of a strain. Tim read voraciously, and when he was interested in a subject the sky was the limit. At such times, when his knowledge and understanding threatened to outstrip his teachers', Clare could appreciate their resentment and frustration. Sometimes *she* felt more like the child than the mother. Right now, for example, she'd love to escape for an hour or so to stretch her legs. The structural renovations now completed, the interior decorators had moved in. The three guest suites in the main lodge were empty for the duration, but there were still four of the five guest chalets occupied, and Clare was in the midst of doing the annual accounts. Maths not being her strong point, it was a chore, even with the new computer that Miles had had installed.

'What is it that's so interesting, anyway?' Clare ventured.

'A biography of David Deverenko. Look, here's a picture of him with his first violin.'

Clare looked and couldn't help but smile. It was anything but a flattering portrait. The young Deverenko looked as if he wanted to break the violin over the head of the photographer. The thick black hair was unruly, and the scowl on his face fierce as he glared at the camera. The violin tucked under his chin almost seemed to grow out of his body. Leave me alone, the glower seemed to say. Can't you see I'm busy? Just so did Tim look when someone tried to interrupt his practice. Clare's eyes flicked to the caption beneath the photograph. Five. Even at five there seemed to be an energy about the small boy that was too big for the confines of the small black and white photograph. She sympathised with his mother. The bear cub must have been hell to tame.

She took the book from Tim and firmly closed it. It had been two months since their personal encounter with Tim's idol, whose poster now hung alongside that of a Stradivarius violin on his bedroom wall. There was no avoiding the man. If Tim wasn't talking about him or reading about him, he was listening to Deverenko recordings on the ghetto-blaster he had saved up for by walking Miles's dogs and helping Grace Cooper in the kitchen.

'You've been reading all morning,' she said. 'It's time you did something else.'

'Why?'

'Because I say so.' She had found it useless to give him an answer he could reason with, if she wanted his rapid obedience. Tim was capable of procrastinating forever when he chose.

'But I don't want to go outside.'

'Fine. Then you can help me. I can't get a program to run on the computer. You can come and tell me what I'm doing wrong.'

'Oh, Mum!' Tim's groan was contemptuous, but Clare could see that he was secretly pleased. Tim was fascinated by computers, but Clare had refused to even consider buying him one, instead putting him off by suggesting he save for one. Tim was such a solitary child already that she didn't want to give him any more excuses to retreat further into his private inner world. First he must learn to relate to *people*. However gifted he was, if he couldn't form stable relationships in later life he would be condemned to a loneliness that Clare couldn't bear to contemplate.

Sure enough, Tim found the problem and ran the program for her, and as a reward Clare let him work on a program he was constructing for himself. She worked on spread sheets at her desk in the large, high-ceilinged office just off the main foyer of the lodge until lunch, which she and Tim ate in the kitchen along with Shari, the live-in maid, and her husband Kerry who acted as general handyman. Grace produced one of her superb game soups, grumbling all the while about the extra work providing meals and snacks for the painters involved. Those at the kitchen table exchanged grins. Grace wouldn't be Grace without a complaint on her lips. She had been cook at the lodge since it had been a private home, and was commonly acknowledged to be one of the best game chefs in Rotorua. She considered Moonlight her home, and looked on the paying guests as family. Since many of them were regulars, 'invited' by Miles—celebrities, politicians, minor royalty and heads of state to whom the tranquillity and unpretentious luxury of Moonlight were a welcome escape from the pressures of the limelight—Grace made it a point to know all their foibles, while at the same time resolutely ignoring them. It was a measure of her culinary reputation, and her bad temper, that *no one* who stayed at Moonlight ever sent a dish back to the kitchen. Clare had seen more than one ruthless tycoon choke down a dish of tripe, or hide spinach in their napkins to dump in the bush later, rather than risk Grace's wrath. At sixty-four, she looked like everybody's kindly old grandmother, but those who had heard her bark agreed that it was only if you had a grandmother who was a Dobermann!

It was a sore point with Grace that the chalets had self-contained kitchens so that guests who wanted complete privacy didn't have to eat in the dining-room at the lodge, but rare was the visitor who, having once sampled Grace's delights, settled for doing their own cooking. The fact that they had two such rarities in residence at the moment had really given Grace something to get her teeth into. George Taverner was a prolific but reclusive writer of action-adventure stories, and whenever he was in danger of not meeting a deadline he holed up at Moonlight, living mainly on whisky, cigarettes and sheer nerves until the book was finished. Clare had seen so little of him, even though he had stayed at Moonlight on and off for about six months during her time there, that she doubted she would even recognise him.

Their other rarity was a famous television face who had slipped discreetly into the country for a break from a gruelling Hollywood work schedule. He, too, was largely an unseen presence, but for a very different reason: a reason that was tall, red-headed, and built like a male fantasy. 'I'll bet that floosie never boiled an egg in her life,' Grace had growled. 'Did you see the order they sent in? *Cans!* They're over there eating out of cans! And they won't even let Shari in to tidy up.'

'Perhaps they're on a secret honeymoon,' said Kerry, straight-faced.

'Like last year, you mean?' his wife had grinned. 'When he was here with the brunette?'

Clare imagined what a field day a gossip columnist could have, eavesdropping on a conversation in the Moonlight kitchen, but it was in the nature of the place that no one had ever broken the trust that the guests placed in their exclusive hideaway. Because the staff was so small, it was necessarily close-knit.

Tim finally succumbed to persuasion after lunch, and went out for a walk with a long-suffering look at his mother that was very adult: he was only doing this for her sake. For her sake he might even try to *enjoy* it. Probably he would come across some animal or insect or fern, and spend the whole time studying it closely, ignoring the frisking of three boisterous dogs.

Clare was arranging flowers in the lounge when she heard the helicopter, and a few minutes later she went out to greet Miles, returning after flying an English industrialist and his wife back to Auckland after a two-week stay.

'Miss me?' He grinned at her as he strode up the stone steps and filled the foyer with his booming voice.

'I hardly had time to,' she said drily. 'You seem to flit about like a butterfly these days, never here long enough to do any work and never away long enough for *us* to get any peace and quiet.'

Miles laughed. He was a big man, as boisterous as his dogs, who thrived on his peripatetic life-style. A keen hunter, he prided himself on his fitness and looked a good deal younger than his fifty years.

'You're too young for peace and quiet, Clare. That's why I've brought you some more guests. First-timers.' He rubbed his hands.

'I thought we'd agreed to delay any more bookings until after the kitchen was finished,' said Clare. 'Couldn't you have put them off for another week?'

'Don't you worry about Gracie. This guy's a gourmet. Wait till you see who it is.'

His enthusiasm was like that of a small boy. Clare had to admit that Miles was a genius at 'picking up' guests...creaming them from the Regent or ringing his mates at the Beehive whenever a state visit was touted. The lodge never advertised; it never had to. Miles's roaming around the globe and his many business interests generated word of mouth recommendations that ensured exclusivity. And naturally all guests had to pass the Parrish test of suitability—i.e. Miles had to like them; mere fame and money didn't provide an entrée.

'OK, but they'll have to take chalet five and it doesn't have any heating yet.' Their heat came from a thermal bore, and the renovations had necessitated relaying some of the pipes.

'There's only two of them; let them have my suite. I'm off to Wellington in a couple of days, and I'll be gone a week. One of the new suites will be ready by then, won't it? What are the bookings like?'

'How long do these new friends of yours want to stay? We're full up from the end of the month.'

Miles shrugged rather sheepishly. 'I don't know...a week or so, I suppose, I forgot to ask. I was so keen for him to come...'

It *must* be someone impressive...either that, or someone who shared his obsession with hunting and fishing. Miles was usually blasé about his guests. Clare shook her head. 'Sometimes, Miles, I wonder how on earth you managed before I came along.'

'So do I,' agreed Miles, although they both knew that one of the secrets of his success was his talent for delegation. He draped a casual arm across her shoulders, hugging her against him as he drew her towards the door to greet the guests who were following a suitcase-laden Kerry up the steps. 'You won't ever leave me, will you, honey? Hell, I'll even make an honest woman of you if you really twist my arm...' He trailed off suggestively, and Clare pinkened at the compliment rather than the implication that their relationship was in any way *dis-*

honest. Miles was the quintessential bachelor; his affection for women, *all* women, as expansive as his
manner. The idea of his settling down was so ludicrous
that he expected everyone to know that he was joking
to even hint at it. If the new guests had got the wrong
impression, they would soon be disabused——

Clare stopped short, riveted by the sight of the man
at the top of the steps.

'Well, I guess you two don't need any introduction,'
said Miles, looking smugly from one to the other.

'No, indeed,' murmured David Deverenko blandly.
'Hello again, Clare.'

'What are you doing here?' asked Clare faintly, aware
of an embarrassing sense of *déjà vu* as she eased herself
from Miles's friendly embrace.

'Isn't it great? Don't you love my surprise?' Miles demanded. 'I called in on Virginia with your messages,
and she told me Davey here was in town and looking
for somewhere to relax for a while before he cranks up
for his next tour...'

Davey? Clare felt a small shock of betrayal. Was the
man *everybody's* friend—except hers? She looked at him
accusingly, and he gave a helpless shrug, as if to ask,
'Can I help it if I'm irresistible?' *Yes.* It had been two
months...she had thought she was *safe*.

'I wouldn't have thought that this was your kind of
place,' she said stiffly. 'I mean, I remember reading
somewhere that you don't approve of hunting or fishing
for sport.'

'Been looking me up?' Deverenko asked innocently,
and she remembered something else. The comment had
been made in an exclusive interview with the author of
his biography, which she had guiltily dipped into in a
spare moment after lunch. She held his gaze with difficulty, her eyes going smoky with the effort of con-
trolling a blush.

Thankfully Miles got her off the hook. 'Where's Tim?
School?'

'It's Saturday, Miles,' said Clare drily. Every day was a work day to her boss; the two were indivisible as far as he was concerned. 'Tim is out with the dogs.'

'Oh. Well, at least I'll get to spring my surprise twice! Look, Clare, you check Davey in and I'll get Shari to give my suite a quick once-over while I collect a few things.' Miles's needs were simple: he tended to live out of a suitcase even at home. 'You'll be on the staff side of the lodge, but only for a few days,' he explained to the dark man who was still watching Clare give a good imitation of being cool and collected, 'and you'll have all the private facilities that you'd have in a guest suite. I have a few things to get on with, so I'll see you later...'

Ignoring the impulse to follow him, Clare braced herself. 'Come into the office and I'll find the book.' Unfortunately the first book that sprang to sight was the glossy Deverenko biography on top of a filing cabinet. She bustled over and heaped a pile of spread sheets over it before she searched out the register. Deverenko didn't say a word, but when she looked up at him there was an amused gleam in his eye that told her he had seen the book and drawn his own egotistical conclusions.

She wished he wouldn't stare so. His eyes were like magnets, drawing her awareness, interfering with her concentration. She sat down at the desk and opened the register. In her hurry to get him out of the room, which suddenly seemed small and airless, she rapped out the necessary questions like a police interrogator.

'And how long do you wish to stay?' she asked, with pen poised over the book. All this was duplicated on the computer but, given the famous names that appeared on its pages, the register was in the nature of an institution, an autograph book crammed with parting comments, both witty and prosaic.

'How long can you put us up...or should that be, put up with us?' he countered, and for the first time Clare became aware of his companion. Deverenko's magnetic aura had been so strong that nothing else had registered.

'I . . . no more than three weeks,' she said, looking at the figure hovering in the doorway, an uncomfortable tightness easing in her throat as she noted that it wasn't a woman but a lanky adolescent. She forced her fingers to relax around the pen. So what if he *had* come with a woman friend, a lover? It would have been nothing to her! 'But surely you won't want to stay that long, anyway?'

'Trying to get rid of me already, Clare?' Deverenko murmured chidingly. 'What would your . . . *employer* . . . say about that?' He was leaning on the desk, his shaggy head almost level with hers. In a soft grey sweater, shabby with age but definitely angora and therefore no doubt hideously expensive, and dark rubbed-corduroy jeans, he looked most unlike the elegant figure he had cut at his concert, and the party afterwards. He looked much more earthy, accessible . . . much more *dangerous* . . .

'My *employer*——' she laid the same emphasis he had on the word, denying him the answer to his subtle question about her relationship with Miles '—leaves the running of Moonlight to me.'

'So we're *your* guests, rather than his. We shall know who to look to for our comfort and well-being . . .'

'Just the two of you?' Clare asked hurriedly, transferring her gaze to the sulky-looking boy in the doorway again.

'Just the two of us,' Deverenko confirmed, turning and extending a hand. 'I should have introduced you. Clare, this is Tamara, my daughter. Tamara, this is Clare Malcolm, Tim's mother . . .'

Ah, that relegates me to my proper place—of secondary interest to my son, thought Clare wryly as she coped with the shock. Not a lanky boy, after all, but a gawky, adolescent girl, tall and thin with a punk-inspired crew-cut that didn't at all flatter her square face with its strong nose and jaw and blemished skin. Having seen pictures of Deverenko's wife, Nina, who had been killed in a plane crash four years earlier, Clare felt her heart go out to the girl. Nina Deverenko had been a great beauty—a small, delicate Frenchwoman of Russian extraction, and a fine musician in her own right, a pianist who often used to accompany her husband. Tamara, it seemed, favoured her father in looks, and Clare realised that she had already antagonised the girl with her surprise. Dark, sullen eyes stonily rejected her greeting, while thin shoulders bunched in dislike beneath a scruffy brown leather jacket. She wore jeans like her father, but with none of his panache.

After mumbling a few words which could have been anything, the girl turned her sullen face towards her father and asked him something in a language that Clare couldn't identify. Her voice was unmusical, oddly rasping, with a faint, whining undertone.

'In English, please, Tamara,' her father corrected her. 'I doubt that Clare understands Russian.'

He would have done better to chastise his daughter for her rudeness in their own language, thought Clare, as she watched the girl's olive complexion darken. Tamara must be at least twelve, but certainly no more than fourteen—not child enough to accept public correction easily, but a long way from being adult enough to accept it gracefully. She was obviously already excruciatingly aware of her own shortcomings, and the inevitable comparisons that her parentage invited.

'I said, what do we have to stay in this *dump* for?' Tamara repeated defiantly. 'I thought this was supposed to be *my* holiday! What are we supposed to do all day, stuck here in the middle of hicksville? According to that old guy, there isn't even a *pool* or TV.'

The 'old guy' being Miles, Clare presumed. 'There's the lake,' she pointed out as she sorted through her drawer to find the extra key to Miles's suite, although people rarely bothered with locked doors at Moonlight.

'And Rotorua's not far away. There's plenty to do and see there.'

'Bor*ing*! Smelly geysers and boiling mud. I've seen it all before and in better places than this.'

Clare recognised the blasé attitude. Few people brought their children to Moonlight—it was an adult retreat—but the ones who did come had a sophistication beyond their years, the natural arrogance of those born to wealth and privilege used to being pandered to in order to gain their parents' favour. Some of them were nice kids under all the gloss, others were already irredeemably spoilt. She wondered which Tamara would turn out to be.

'Why don't you take a wander around and see what there *is* on offer?' her father suggested.

'Why? What are you going to do?' Tamara demanded suspiciously.

'Sign in, and then go and have a lie down in our room,' he told her patiently. 'I still feel jet-lagged from our London flight. You can come and rest, too, if you like.'

'No, thanks.' Tamara revealed she had some manners after all, albeit grudging ones. 'I guess I'll just have a look around and see what there *isn't*.' With a last baleful look at Clare she slouched out. Clare got the impression that, if Deverenko hadn't issued the invitation to rest with him, his daughter would have insisted on sticking by his side.

'I'm sorry.' Deverenko sighed when the sound of the girl's footsteps faded. 'Tamara's going through a difficult stage. I had already planned to come down here when she ... got some extra time off school, so I had no choice but to bring her ...'

Suspended, thought Clare, reading between the lines of his unease and Tamara's defiance. 'You hadn't booked,' she pointed out. 'Surely you could have postponed your visit? I would have thought your first obligation was towards your daughter...' Her voice trailed off as the dark gaze narrowed on her face.

'So it is, but she has to learn that she can't manipulate me as easily as she seems to manipulate her teachers. I hadn't booked, Clare, because I wouldn't have put it past you to go off on holiday yourself if you found out I was coming down. Virginia said that with the renovations going on she didn't think I'd have any trouble persuading Miles to invite me down.'

The answer to her unasked question was the one she had expected.

'And just why *are* you here, Mr Deverenko? And don't tell me it's just to relax between tours!'

'If you can't call me David, you'd better settle for a deferential "maestro",' he taunted her excessive politeness. 'Since you seem too in awe of me to treat me like a normal human being.'

'You still haven't answered my question, *David*.'

'All in good time. Aren't you going to show me to my room? I meant it when I said I was tired.'

'Yes, of course,' Clare said automatically, handing him his key and showing him out of the office. Actually, he did look rather worn. There were shadows beneath his dark eyes and a slight hollowness to his cheeks that had not been there the last time she'd seen him. Some of his exuberant vitality was missing, or at least dimmed. 'When did you arrive from London?' she asked, as they traversed the foyer and turned down the narrow, echoing hallway which led to the staff wing of the sprawling lodge.

'The day before yesterday. I'm used to air travel, it usually doesn't affect me too much, but we were doing some recording in London as well as the concerts, and I had two engagements in New York to fit in, thanks to the curse of Concorde. I have an American tour coming up next month, so I told Efrem—he's my manager—to extricate me from any minor engagements until then. I'm not as young as I used to be, and I refuse to perform the miracles I did when I was twenty... I'm thirty-five,' he offered her sidelong assessment.

'You look older,' she told him as she opened the door to Miles's twin-bedroomed suite.

He chuckled. 'Is that the truth, or are you just trying to emphasise your disapproval of me? What have I done, Clare, besides avail myself of your hospitality, to make you dislike me so?'

'I don't dislike you; I don't know you.'

'That's why I'm here.'

'What?' She swung around from her pretence of surveying the spick and span lounge.

Deverenko tossed his keys on to a kauri coffee-table and strolled across to look out the window at the splendid view of the glassy lake. 'You were right. You accused me of presumption, of making judgements about you and Tim without knowing anything about you. I'm here to remedy that.'

His dark eyes were a challenge that Clare didn't dare meet. 'You and I got off on the wrong foot—partly my fault, partly yours. But I don't think Tim should suffer because of *our* differences——'

'Tim's not *suffering*——'

'Sorry, poor choice of words. I mean, before either of us make a final decision about the other, I think we should get to know each other with open minds. Mmm?'

The prospect was appalling. Clare could feel herself begin to blush and turned away, but not quickly enough for his observant eye.

'Do I embarrass you? I don't mean to. The intimacy I suggest is intellectual rather than physical. You would not be compromising your position with your...er... employer.'

'My lover, you mean!' she was goaded by his delicacy to snap.

'Do I? Are you lovers...you and the "old guy", to borrow my daughter's phraseology?'

'That's none of your business.'

'It would be if Miles Parrish had some stake in Tim's future. If, for example, he were to become the boy's stepfather.'

'Miles and I are not contemplating marriage at this time,' she clipped, still holding out the protective possibility. 'But even if we were, any decision about Tim would be *mine*.'

'Is that fair? Not to share the responsibility for him? Does not the family unit depend for its stability on all members sharing equal love and responsibility? Otherwise there can be conflict and resentment. Both natural and stepchildren should surely be treated equally.'

Clare ran a nervous hand through her hair, tucking it back behind her ear and then flicking it forward again when he stared at the exposed curve of her neck. 'How did we get into this ridiculously hypothetical discussion?' she asked shakily, wishing she wasn't so self-conscious in his presence.

'I was trying to find out whether you were serious about Miles Parrish. Does he know about this kissing cousin of yours in Auckland with whom you wrestle in gardens?'

Clare's mouth made a little 'O'. He was making her sound like a promiscuous tart—she who had never looked at another man since Lee had died! The dimple quivered on the verge of discovery, and her hand came up to depress it.

He was laughing at her. 'I am terrible, no? You are interested in neither of these two men. You only dally with them. The thought of anything serious makes you want to laugh.'

'No, it's your words that make me want to laugh,' she said quellingly. 'You speak better English than I do, so why do you put on this mock-Russian accent?'

'Habit. People expect it. They find it endearing.'

'Well, I merely find it irritating.'

'You find *me* irritating?' he suggested.

'Yes!'

He tilted his head to one side. 'But it is an interesting friction, no?' he said slyly, his accent so thick you could stand a spoon in it. 'It makes one tingle in such unexpected places...'

Clare could feel herself blushing again, as much at the wicked look in his eye as at the infuriating accuracy of his remark. She hurried over and threw open the bedroom doors. 'Both rooms have en suite bathrooms and there's a small kitchenette for making tea and coffee but no cooking facilities. If you need maid service you can dial Shari on 002. 001 will give you an outside line, and the switchboard is computerised so you can direct-dial your toll calls if you like and they'll be automatically added to your bill. We can arrange any tours you like. The fishing season here has ended, but we can arrange a trip to Taupo if you want to fish, and we have several guides on call for hunting——'

'And what number do I dial to call you?' Deverenko was studying the card by the telephone in the lounge. Miles had a fetish for phones, and they were scattered liberally around the lodge. Suddenly he found it and began to laugh. 'I'm not surprised. 007. Do you have a secret hankering for a life packed with danger, sex and gratuitous brand-names?'

'It was Miles's idea,' she said repressively.

'Of course, heaven forbid you should admit to such whimsicality yourself.' His teasing was interrupted by a savage yawn.

'You should be in bed,' she said automatically, and was suddenly visited by an unexpected vision of that compact, muscular body sprawled across Miles's big double bed, all that aggressive maleness dissipated in the little-boy innocence of sleep.

'I know. I feel like I'm sleep-walking. What's the arrangement about meals here?'

'Dinner is at eight, but if you can't be bothered dressing you can have it served here.'

He pulled a tired face. 'How dressed does one have to be?'

'Not formal, if that's what you mean. People who come here to stay are generally trying to escape that sort of routine. We're pretty casual. Breakfast is at eight, lunch at one, but any time you're hungry you can get a snack from the kitchen—providing you go there yourself. Grace—she's our cook—likes to see who she's feeding. It's a help-yourself bar, too, except in the evening when Kerry's there. The key to the wine-cellar is behind the bar—whatever you take, just write it down and leave it on the spike under the counter.'

'Heavens, how does this place make money?' he conquered another yawn to ask.

'Wait until you see your bill,' Clare dimpled. 'You're going to be paying through the nose for the privilege of getting to know me.'

The dark eyes blinked at her with sleepy amusement. 'That appeals to you, doesn't it? Well, I have no objection. I'm a fairly wealthy man... and I *always* make sure I get value for my money. So just be warned, Clare. If I suspect I'm being screwed for your entertainment, I may well decide to return the favour.'

It seemed, for a moment, that the double entendre had gone right over the top of her innocent head, and he began to laugh. Then her frown was swamped by a wild blush that touched him with tender remorse. The little pink bow of her mouth trembled as she attempted to frame her outrage and he hastened to apologise.

'I'm sorry, Clare, put it down to fatigue...I shouldn't have added crudity to my sins against you, but you blush more exquisitely than any woman I know. I can be a brute and a pig when I'm tired. Actually, I have the utmost respect for you.'

'A simple sorry would have done. You don't have to lay it on with a trowel,' said Clare acerbically, recovering her poise.

'Then I'm forgiven?' he asked gravely.

She looked into melting dark eyes and felt a tiny tug, deep inside. This man reminded her too much of what it meant to be a woman, and a shy and inexperienced one at that.

'Certainly not.' She turned on her heel and left.

His startled laughter pursued her into the hall. It sounded like the soft ripping of silk, appropriately so, thought Clare as she fled back to the safety of her work. David Deverenko seemed intent on tearing a large hole in the carefully worked fabric of her life. Already he had unravelled a few threads. If he knew how really vulnerable she was, she would be lost. At all costs, she must maintain her assured front.

And the first thing she must do was to learn how not to blush!

CHAPTER FOUR

TO TIM'S great disappointment neither Deverenko nor his daughter were at dinner that night; but the next morning, when Clare called into the kitchen on her way to breakfast, she found him there sipping coffee and chatting to Grace as if they were old friends. It was a crisp, cold morning, and Clare's manner was equally cool. She had been caught by surprise yesterday, but today she was fully in control of all her responses and she returned Deverenko's greeting with the same calm hospitality she extended to all the guests at the lodge.

'Did you sleep well?' she enquired automatically, accepting Grace's offer of a fragrant cup of coffee.

'Beautifully. I feel completely refreshed, and once Grace feeds me I shall be utterly at peace with the world.'

'The sooner you let me alone to get on with my work, the sooner you'll get fed,' said Grace in her usual abrupt way, and Deverenko grinned.

'Certainly, Grace. My apologies for getting in your way. Come along, Clare.' He took her coffee out of her hand and carried the two cups out into the hall. 'Which way to the dining-room?'

Clare led the way. The dining-room was a long, narrow room along the front of the lodge. Every table had a window-seat, overlooking the lake, and french doors at regular intervals along the room opened out to a veranda where, weather permitting, the guests could have their meals. Early-morning mist wreathed the lake, making alfresco dining an unappealing prospect, and Clare showed Deverenko to a table at the far end of the room where the weak morning sunlight added to the warmth of the room. The thick beige carpet and natural wood panelling on the walls and exposed-beam ceilings

were the same throughout the lodge, creating the kind
of spartan luxury that Moonlight was famous for.

'Aren't you going to join me? Grace told me that it's
accepted practice for staff and guests to dine together,'
he said smoothly, as Clare retrieved her coffee and began
to turn away.

'I...thought that you and your daughter might prefer
to eat alone,' ventured Clare hopefully.

'Tamara has ordered breakfast in bed.'

Still hovering, trying to think of a good reason to
refuse his invitation, she offered him a meaningless smile.
'I suppose she's at the age to discover that just because
you wake up, it doesn't mean you have to *get* up.'

'I rather think it's more of a case of wanting the opposite of what her father wants,' he said wryly. 'Her way
of making sure I don't take her for granted.' Clare still
hovered, and his dark eyes fell to the small menu con-
sideringly as he added casually, 'Also to punish me for
spending so long with your son this morning. He came
to visit and welcome us to the lodge.'

Clare sat down with a thump, her coolness compro-
mised by annoyed embarrassment. 'Did he wake you?
I'm terribly sorry. I did *tell* him he wasn't to annoy
you...'

'He didn't annoy me in the least, and I was already
awake when he knocked——'

'Still, he knows he isn't supposed to disturb
guests——'

'Relax, Clare, I told you, I didn't mind. I enjoyed
talking with him again.' Deverenko picked up another
menu and put it in her hands. 'And, after all, I'm not
the normal type of guest. I came down here to see you
and Tim. He at least was pleased to see me. In fact,
come to think of it, it was Tim who suggested I come
to Moonlight, so I guess he feels a proprietorial interest
in looking after me.'

Clare pretended to be studying the menu she knew off
by heart, having typed it herself, while she resolutely

fought a blush. She was definitely going to have a talk with Tim! When she felt confident that she had defeated the advance of blood to her cheeks, she looked up again. Deverenko was studying her expression with vague disappointment. Clare's confidence rose. He had *deliberately* tried to embarrass her for his own entertainment.

'I can recommend the fish with melon.'

'I'll have that, then,' he said, tossing aside his menu, giving up his own pretence of interest. 'Would you object, Clare, if while I'm here I give Tim a few lessons?'

'I suppose you've already mentioned the possibility to him, so the question is rather redundant,' said Clare tightly.

'No, I haven't. I wouldn't be so underhand.'

'Really?' Clare's scepticism made his muscles along his jaw tighten aggressively.

'Really. It's up to you. But I should say this: Tim will probably ask me to hear him, and I won't lie about my interest for your sake.'

'As I said, the question is rather redundant, then. Just don't go making any more statements about him to the Press.'

'You never let me explain about that.'

Clare was about to make a curt reply when they were interrupted by Grace asking whether they'd made up their minds about their choice. Normally Grace's niece, Trina, did the waitressing, but Miles had given her her annual holidays while the lodge was semi-closed for the alterations. Grace wouldn't let Deverenko get away with a single course, and bullied him into starting with a terrine of fresh fruit and finishing with her 'special' coffee, the recipe for which was a closely guarded secret.

'If I stay here too long, I'll run to fat,' said Deverenko with the carelessness of one who knew it wasn't true.

'Just think of the advantages. If you grow a double chin, you won't need a chin-rest on your violin, you can just tuck it into the rolls of fat. You're fairly solid now.' Clare allowed her eyes to run over him critically.

He stiffened. 'I have an artist's discipline. I would never allow myself to be overweight. It's my Russian heritage—strong bones and solid flesh. To be a violinist requires endurance and fitness; this is muscle, not fat.' He flexed an arm to show her.

Clare could believe it. Her long lashes hid her satisfaction at his annoyance. He had a very healthy ego, but he was obviously as much a perfectionist personally as he was professionally, and thus sensitive to any hint of serious criticism.

'If you say so,' she said meekly, and there was a brief silence in which she thought she might have gone too far. But, if he guessed she had been leading him on, he did not say so. Instead he returned to the conversation they had been having before the interruption.

'To set the record straight, Clare, I didn't make any statement as such to that reporter; I merely agreed with his assessment that Tim showed extraordinary capability for his age. I refused to make any further comment. I was something of a prodigy myself, as you may know, and I realise the damage that intrusive publicity can do, the unfair expectations it can create.'

'I see,' Clare murmured, unable to bring herself to apologise for her misconception. She badly needed the barriers that her resentment had created. At close quarters his personality was oppressively warm. Relaxed and male, he looked very much at home in his surroundings, as if he belonged there, across the table, her breakfast companion.

'So, I have your permission for the lessons?'

'Of course. As long as they don't interfere with his schoolwork or regular lessons.'

'I should like to meet his teacher.'

'I'm sure she'd be thrilled to meet you,' said Clare with dry resignation. It was an understatement, and they both knew it. Cheryl Tyson would be over the moon at a personal introduction to one of the world's great violinists.

'I'll be delighted to meet her,' Deverenko said with a demureness that didn't suit him.

'I don't doubt it. She's small and dark and rather beautiful.'

'I prefer blondes with legs that go on forever,' said Deverenko with an innocence that had Clare choking in her orange juice.

'Your wife was a brunette,' she pointed out when she had recovered.

'Nina was an aberration...' The light flirtatiousness took on the warmth of reminiscence. 'A much-loved aberration.'

'I heard her play once, with the NZSO. She was marvellous.'

'Mmm. For a while, after she died, some of the music died with her, but she would have hated that. She hated me to be anything less than I could be. She was a perfect partner for those struggling years.' He appeared lost in thought for a few minutes—then, as he attacked his terrine with gusto, he said, 'So you went to a concert of Nina's and enjoyed it. I'm glad at least *one* of my family managed not to bore you to sleep during a performance.'

This time the blush couldn't be withheld and he chuckled, but his humour had a slightly malicious edge to it that told her he was truly offended.

'Oh, so you noticed...'

'Yes, I noticed. It was difficult not to: you were practically in the front row and your snores had the first violins fighting to keep tempo.'

'I wasn't snoring!' cried Clare, appalled at the possibility.

'And the boyfriend whose lap you were draped across was so busy leering down your cleavage that I doubt he heard a note, either.'

'He wasn't my boyfriend. I'd never seen him before. You only gave us three tickets, remember.'

'Then all I can say is that you allow strangers a great deal of latitude with your person. Next time you go to a concert, wear a high-necked dress. I suppose I should be thankful that you didn't come complete with Walkman to enliven the leaden evening.'

'I told you, I was tired——' She was about to placate his bruised sensibilities by telling him about her wretched flu, when Tim found them.

'Good morning, Mr Deverenko,' he said, as he slid his slight form into the seat beside his mother.

Clare opened her mouth to remonstrate with him for his early morning call, and then closed it again when she caught the faint shake of Deverenko's head.

'Have you told Grace what you want?' she asked instead.

'Of course I have.' Tim gave her an impatient look. 'What are you going to do today?' he asked the dark man who was studying mother and son together.

'Give the man a chance, Tim. He hasn't had his breakfast yet.'

'I thought you might have some suggestions,' said Deverenko. 'I've done the tourist route in Rotorua before, and I thought you might be able to recommend something a little different that doesn't involve too many other people.'

'Miles could take you hunting,' suggested Clare meanly.

'He doesn't want to *hunt*,' scorned Tim. 'He doesn't like hunting. He's a conservationist, aren't you, Mr Deverenko? It's in the book...that one you took off me, Mum, the one you were looking at——'

Clare avoided laughing brown eyes, hoist with her own petard.

'We could go out on the lake, though. Miles has this neat luxury launch.'

Clare winced inwardly at the 'we'. 'Mr Deverenko has his daughter with him, Tim. They're here to spend some time together.' It wouldn't hurt to let Tim know that he didn't have first claim on his hero's attention. 'He and Tamara may not want anyone else along.'

'He and Tamara would welcome the buffer,' said Deverenko blandly, as if he knew her fingers were crossed under the table. 'But three is an awkward number. If we go out, I think it would be better if both you *and* your mother come along with us.'

'I do have some work to do,' Clare murmured, and found herself the focus of two sets of reproachful eyes.

'On a Sunday?' Deverenko asked.

'A hotel is a hotel every day of the week,' Clare pointed out.

'Don't you want to come?' asked Tim bluntly, and Clare quailed slightly under that direct regard. Trust Tim to cut to the heart of the matter with childishly adult perception! 'Why?'

'Yes, Clare, why?' Deverenko gently mimicked her son's question, leaning back in his chair, flustering her with his knowing smile.

'Don't encourage him,' she snapped.

'To be enquiring?' he wilfully misunderstood her. 'I have an enquiring mind myself. For instance, I begin to wonder why you're so reluctant to relax in my company. What are you afraid will happen if you do?'

Conscious of Tim's grave curiosity, Clare strove to appear amused. 'Perhaps I'm just awed by your august presence.'

'You hide it well. People in awe of me usually bow and scrape. But perhaps you're like my daughter in that respect: offence is the best defence. You're at your most bold when you're at your most insecure...'

It was such a terrifyingly apt assessment that Clare instantly regained her poise. 'Then Tamara *must* be in dire need of the reassurance of your attention. Perhaps you had better turn your enquiring mind to identifying her needs rather than those of perfect strangers——' She stopped as he gave a short, growling laugh, realising that she had just confirmed his statement with her attack.

'Mum?' She also realised that Tim was disturbed by the subtle undertones in the exchange. No more disturbed than she!

'It's all right, Tim,' to her chagrin it was Deverenko who eased the moment, 'your mother and I are just teasing each other, aren't we, Clare?' She gave a weak smile. 'If I promise to be good, will you come with us? If I promise to be very, *very* good?'

The sexual boast implicit in the innocent phrase was revealed in the wickedness of his attractive smile. Clare's feminine instinct told her that it was no idle boast, either. There was an animal vitality about him that she found both attractive and repellent, hinting as it did of a sensual appetite that was alien to her experience. She had loved Lee, but due to her reserve and Lee's tender protectiveness there had been no wild excitement in their sexual relationship, although it had been warm and completely fulfilling to the woman she had been. She didn't welcome the thought that she might have changed since his death, that she might have physical desires unrelated to her emotional need for security.

Later that morning, helping Kerry unload the groaning hamper and stock the fridge in the small galley of the launch, Clare wondered if she would have had the strength to continue to resist the dual pleas if Miles hadn't come into the dining-room at that moment and swept all before his enthusiasm.

'Great! Great!' he boomed when Deverenko told him of the suggestion. 'The launch could do with a run— waste of money just sitting there. Drive you myself— blow a few cobwebs away—make a day of it. And if you don't mind, Davey, I'll ask Doug Fallon to tag along— he needs a few lake shots of the lodge for his book.' He explained that Doug was a wildlife photographer of international repute, working on a book which combined travel information for birdwatchers with studies of New Zealand birds in their natural habitats. Doug was the other chalet occupant, usually absent at breakfast because he spent his nights pursuing the elusive kiwi with his lens and generally never surfaced until noon.

Clare's feeble protestations of work had been over-ridden, and Deverenko had tipped her a smug smile as he had gone off to inform Tamara of the scheme. If his daughter was intent on being difficult, Clare wondered what technique Deverenko would use to convince her to join them, but when she waved Kerry off the boat and watched the newest guests walk down from the lodge to the long wooden jetty she had her answer. It was Deverenko who was lagging, hands thrust sullenly in his jeans pockets while his daughter, inappropriately dressed in a bright red dress that, although long-sleeved, looked very thin and more suited to a shopping expedition than a winter boat ride, strode haughtily ahead. Clare turned away to hide her rueful smile. She had used such child psychology herself, pretending reluctance to encourage interest, although she and Tim were so attuned that it was becoming increasingly difficult to fool him.

Doug Fallon, tall, blond and softly-spoken, was the last to arrive, loaded down with camera bags. Clare helped him store them while Deverenko, Tamara and Tim joined Miles on the top deck as he switched on the engines and spun the wheel to ease the sleek blue and white launch away from the jetty. When Doug was ready, he called up instructions to Miles and leaned over the bow rail to take his shots. The original sixty-year-old homestead that formed the basis of the lodge was constructed in weathered stone, and the extensions made over the years were in the same stone. Nestling in the bush, the wooden chalets almost out of sight among the trees, Moonlight looked like a natural outgrowth of the lava rock that formed the shores of the lake. Lake Romata was on the northern edge of Rotorua's volcanic centre, the highest of the mosaic of lakes in the region created by massive eruptions and lava flows over hundreds of thousands of years. Although Romata had none of the geysers and mudpools and spectacular thermal effects that drew tourists to other lakes in the Rotorua region, Clare thought its peace and beauty a joy in itself. Because there was no road right around the lake, most of the native bush was unspoiled—small, secluded beaches around the shoreline a delight to discover only by boat. The lake was very deep and correspondingly cold and brilliant of colour, and on days like today, when there was little breeze, reflected bush and sky with mirror-like clarity.

After Doug had got the shots he wanted, Miles aimed the launch at the far shore and Deverenko allowed Tim to show him the galley and cabins below. Tamara, who was obviously having second thoughts about the whole thing, looked for a moment as if she might join them, but then flounced over to one of the deck-chairs and sat down, a picture of boredom. Clare joined her with a sigh.

'You don't have to sit with me, you know. I don't need a baby-sitter,' the girl said in a hard little voice. 'I know where you really want to be.'

'Oh? Where's that?' asked Clare in surprise. Had Deverenko told her of Clare's reluctance to come, as part of his psychology?

'With my father. All the women drool over him. Only he doesn't want any of them, so you're wasting your time if you think he'd be interested in *you*.' Tamara's dark brown eyes slid insolently over Clare's warmly track-suited figure, well-padded against the cold. Although the sun was shining, its rays were weak, and Clare knew that if it clouded over the temperature over the lake could drop quickly and markedly.

'Have you been to Rotorua before?' asked Clare, deciding to ignore her rudeness.

'Of course I have. I used to go *everywhere* with Mum and Dad. I've been all over the world.'

'What about your schooling?'

'I had tutors.'

'But you're at school now?'

The question didn't go down well. 'I was for a while.' She named a very prestigious English girls' school. 'But I've left. I'm going to be going on tour with Dad from now on.' She looked challengingly at Clare, as if she would welcome a chance to argue.

'You're very lucky. I've never been out of New Zealand. I planned to save up and travel when I became a secretary, after I left school, but I met Lee and got married instead. We did travel around New Zealand a lot, though.' Clare smiled. 'Touring, like your dad.'

'Your husband was a musician?' Tamara demanded narrowly.

'He was lead guitarist and vocalist with a rock band, Kraken.'

'Never heard of them,' Tamara carelessly dismissed.

'I guess you wouldn't have,' said Clare mildly, 'if you haven't been in New Zealand much. They were only just achieving a following when Lee died and the band broke up. Their last hit was a couple of years ago.' The record company had shrewdly released the album just after Lee's death, and taken great advantage of the resultant publicity. Clare hadn't agreed with Virginia's accusation that it had been a morbid, mercenary act. She had preferred to look on the *Myth* album as a very fitting memorial to a very talented man. That Lee was the driving force and inspiration for the band was confirmed when Kraken had disbanded seven months later without having produced another record.

'I'm going down to bring out a few drinks and snacks,' Clare said, getting up after a few more abortive attempts at conversation. 'Would you like to come and help me?'

'It's your job, not mine. I'm not a waitress,' Tamara sneered, and Clare had to leave before she made the crushing retort that was on the tip of her tongue. Tamara was obviously a very unhappy girl, intent on taking it out on everyone else.

When Tim and his idol came back on deck, Clare endeavoured to manoeuvre Deverenko into the chair by his

daughter, and got Tim to take a few snacks and a couple
of cold cans of beer to Miles and Doug on the upper
deck—but her efforts were in vain. Tim was not to be
separated for any length of time from the new sun on
his horizon, basking openly in the warmth of his interest.
Clare found herself becoming as tense and quiet as
Tamara. Couldn't Deverenko *see* how much he was al-
ienating his daughter? Why couldn't he make the effort
to include her more in his conversation? No wonder she
felt left out. Clare was feeling left out, too, a very un-
usual occurrence with Tim. Usually it was Clare to whom
he turned for approval; today it was Deverenko.

After creaming lazily around the perimeter of the lake
for a couple of hours, Miles anchored off a small bay
and Clare set out the sumptuous lunch that Grace had
prepared. There were oysters and smoked marlin and
trout, lamb and cashew-nut terrine, lobster salad and a
variety of imaginative sandwiches that would appeal to
young palates, although Clare noticed without much
surprise that Tamara ate the adult fare. At least her
problems didn't include anorexia, for, although her
painful thinness was accentuated by the unflattering
simplicity of the red dress, Tamara's appetite seemed
healthily casual. For dessert there was an ultra-rich kiwi-
fruit cheesecake and plenty of fresh fruit and several
kinds of New Zealand cheese served with plain water
crackers.

They ate on the deck, the food shaded by a blue-and-
white striped awning, watching the ducks, crested grebes
and dabchicks ripple the glassy surface of the lake. Used
to Doug's ever-present camera, Clare didn't take any
notice of the photographs he was taking until Deverenko
held up a hand.

'If you don't mind, I'd rather you didn't include
Tamara and me.' His voice was pleasant, but with enough
of an edge for Doug to lower his camera immediately.

'These aren't for publication, just a few personal
shots.' After an awkward pause, he added, 'You're

welcome to see the pictures. In fact, I'll give you the prints and the negs when I've developed them—I have a temporary dark-room rigged up in my chalet.'

'Thanks, I'd like to have them,' Deverenko said, turning to Miles as they both leaned on the rail. 'Is the launch just for cruising, or can you fish this lake?'

'The fishing season closed at the end of June, otherwise I'd bring you out,' Miles told him. 'There's good trout fishing here, I could guarantee you a Rainbow of a couple of kilos at least. You come back between October and June and I'll show you. We generally use sinking lines to twenty or so metres; the waters around here are pretty deep.'

'I might take you up on that.'

'I thought you didn't like fishing,' frowned Tim. It always disconcerted him to find that his precious books had misled him.

'If I fish, I eat what I catch,' Deverenko told him. 'But I don't get the opportunity very often, and I certainly wouldn't do it as a sport.'

'Most sport fishing is on a tag and release basis,' said Miles, prompting a mild argument on the subject of wildlife management. By the time it wound up, Clare had cleared the lunch debris away, and Miles proposed continuing to the north end of the lake.

'How about taking a turn at the wheel, sport?' Miles asked Tim.

'Not today, thanks, Uncle Miles,' said Tim politely.

'You usually pester the life out of Miles to let you have a go,' Clare protested, looking helplessly at her son.

'Next time, maybe,' he temporised, for all the world like an adult placating an awkward child, and Clare rolled her eyes while Miles laughed and clapped Deverenko on the back.

'You seem to have acquired a shadow, old man.'

Deverenko smiled, and a few minutes later he and Tim were down on the fishing platform at the stern. From the deck, she could see Tim's hands gesturing as he talked.

'What on earth do they find to talk about all the time? Tim's *never* been a chatterer, but now he doesn't seem to be able to stop.'

Her murmur was supposed to be for Doug, but Tamara answered.

'They're talking about music, of course.' Her rough-edged voice was sullen with resentment. The sun had gone behind a cloud, and Clare noticed the way her thin arms were wrapped across her chest.

'Are you cold? There's an extra sweater in the forward cabin if you want one.'

'No, thanks.' I don't need *anyone*'s help, her tone said, and Clare and Doug exchanged glances of silent understanding.

'I'm getting pretty chilly myself,' said Doug. 'I'll go below and get my jacket. I'll bring the sweater back for you, Tamara. We can't have a fellow guest, and a young lady at that, risking a chill. You don't want to be laid low with flu when you're on holiday...'

It was the right touch, referring to her as a fellow guest, and a lady. Tamara gave him a graciously conde-scending smile, and he saluted her with a grin in return.

Clare returned her thoughtful glances to the two backs on the fishing platform, ignoring the silent girl at her side until Tamara was driven to say.

'Your kid is pretty pushy, isn't he?'

'Not usually, no. He's very shy as a rule,' said Clare slowly. 'I've never seen him cling like that to anyone else.' She frowned. That sounded like sour grapes. *Was* she jealous? Did she *want* Tim to cling only to her?

'I told you. It's music. All musicians are the same.'

'Are you? Do you play an instrument?'

'Should I?' Tamara countered, her eyes shiny with dislike, and Clare realised she had made another mistake.

'I don't either,' she tried to redeem herself. 'It's funny, I love music, I love dancing to music, but I never had

the slightest urge to learn to play it. Until now, until I
realised that I couldn't help Tim with his music problems
because I didn't understand them! In every other way
he needs me, but not when he has his violin in his hand.
I suppose I'm afraid of it, in a way, afraid of his talent
because it's not something I can share in... ever, except
second-hand. Sometimes I feel it's like a wall between
us...' She suddenly realised who she was talking to and
turned her head and grimaced. 'I suppose you're going
to accuse me of being a neurotic mother, as your father
has.'

'Dad said *that*?'

'Well, not those exact words, but that's what he
thinks.' She glared down at the figure in the pale
windbreaker.

'You... you really don't like him, do you?' Tamara
realised incredulously.

Clare's mouth curved wryly. Although Tamara had
attempted to put her off her father, it had obviously never
occurred to her that anyone could not be impressed by
him, awed by him as she was. 'Should I? Your father
waltzes into our lives and calmly assures that he can turn
them upside-down without so much as a by your leave,
as if everything is subservient to his talent and will. Well,
I'm *not*, and no amount of pressure from your father
or Tim is going to convince me that his needs are going
to be best served by shipping him off to a boarding-
school. Tim worships your father, but he doesn't realise
that the kind of attention being lavished on him now is
only a means to an end. Once Tim's at the school, how
often will he see your father?'

'More than I saw him at my school,' said Tamara.

'Is that why you left? Because you missed him?'

'I didn't leave, I was asked to leave,' Tamara confirmed Clare's suspicion with a dull defiance. 'They said
I was too disruptive. I ran away three times.'

'Where did you go?' Clare was aghast at the idea.

'To friends. Once I got as far as Rome, on my way to America where Dad was performing,' she said with pride.

'By *yourself*?' It was pointless to hide her shock.

'Sure by myself. I can look after myself. I can look after Dad, too, if he'd let me. He needs someone with him on tour. He gets wound up, you know. Mum used to be great at smoothing things out for him. Now he only has Efrem, and Efrem likes to panic.'

'Efrem?'

'Daddy's manager. He manages some of the top musicians in the world. He's OK, I guess, but he's very American, you know? He fusses and likes rowing... he calls it being full of *temperament*. He drives Daddy mad sometimes.'

'Then why does he employ him?'

Tamara looked shocked. 'Because he's the *best*, of course. You don't *employ* Efrem... he *invites* you to work with him. And he's been with Daddy since he first started the concert circuit. They'll never get *divorced*!'

'You make me feel very plain and ordinary and ignorant,' said Clare ruefully, 'and I can do without another Deverenko who makes me feel inferior.'

'I didn't mean to,' offered Tamara, with a dark-eyed sincerity that was touching, considering her earlier hostility. Perhaps it was the realisation that Clare wasn't 'drooling' over her father that prompted the change. Whatever it was, Clare knew better than to trust it would last, but she would take advantage of it while it existed.

'Nor does your father, most of the time; it just comes naturally.'

Tamara laughed, and the difference in her appearance was quite startling, illuminating her features, rounding out the contours of her square, spare face. 'He is rather bossy, but everyone forgives him because he's special.'

'Everyone is special in their own way, Tamara, even those of us who seem destined to live under the shadow of greatness. I refuse to be intimidated. I can be bossy, too, you know.'

'You don't look very tough.'

'Toughness is on the inside. You look as if a puff of wind could blow you away, but you're a pretty tough cookie yourself.'

Tamara grinned, but Clare saw the flicker in her eyes. Tamara wasn't half as tough as she acted, and she knew it and it frightened her. Clare stood up. It was about time David Deverenko spent some time with his daughter, even if it meant that she, Clare, had to provide the diversion from her son.

The things she did for others!

CHAPTER FIVE

CLARE switched off her blow-dryer and ran her fingers through her clean hair, fluffing out the blunt-cut ends so that it framed her face in a thick bob. She had showered and dusted herself with fragrant talc and put on her nightgown and warm, wine-red robe. Now she intended to relax for the rest of the evening with a good book to ease the restless tension of her day.

It was the fourth day of the Deverenkos' stay at Moonlight, and Clare had found it just as difficult as the previous three. Tim's reluctance to go to school was more marked than usual, although Clare had been un-principled enough to use the bribe of violin lessons with David as she packed him off on the boat each morning in time to catch the school bus which picked him up from the Lake Romata stop on State Highway 86. Today it had been his regular lesson with Cheryl, and when Clare had taken the station wagon—the road was just passable by afternoon—into Rotorua for her 'jazzercise' session at the gym before she ferried Tim to and from his lesson, the Deverenkos had accompanied her. David had gone with Tim to his lesson, while Tamara went to the gym with Clare and watched her join the fifteen or so other women in their energetic dancing. Tamara, who had obviously regretted her confidences of the second day, had thawed slightly as Clare, sweaty from her exertions, had come off the floor.

'You must have to be awfully fit,' she said wistfully. 'We do—did—gym at school, but it was always boring and sport was compulsory. Ugh, I hated it!'

'*I'm* fit, but then I've always danced,' said Clare as they walked towards the changing-rooms. 'But we have new people joining all the time. They just do as much

73

of the routine as they can manage. The important thing is to enjoy it. My working hours are pretty flexible, especially when our bookings are light, so I can come as often, or as little, as I want. Most women find twice a week is enough to keep in shape, especially when they've built up to the full hour session. Maybe you'd like to try it some time.'

Tamara instantly backed off. 'I've never done any dancing or anything. With all our travelling there was never any time for stuff like that...except music lessons, of course.'

And yet she said she didn't play an instrument. Tactfully Clare ignored the tail-end of her remark. 'You don't have to be an expert, the instructor demonstrates everything.' She dimpled mischievously. 'And you notice how I always stay at the back? That's so I can watch everyone else instead of them watching me.' She often wondered whether she would have been able to make a career out of ballet even if it hadn't been physically precluded, given her shyness in front of people, but she hadn't been tempted. Dancing in a gym with a group of friendly women was vastly different from doing it on stage. No, this way Clare had the best of both worlds: she could lose herself in the music and the physical enjoyment of dancing without drawing attention to herself.

'I don't have any of the gear, anyway,' said Tamara, eyeing Clare's slinky purple leotard and blue tights, the pink leg warmers and foreshortened T-shirt she wore.

'All you need is the leotard and tights, and you can hire those from the gym. Do you want to have a go next time, Tamara?'

She shrugged, as if afraid of expressing any eagerness. 'I don't know. Dad might want to do something else.'

'What about what *you* want to do, Tamara?' asked Clare quietly. 'Why don't you forget your father for once, and be responsible for your own enjoyment? It's not as if this is something your father can join in with. It's sexist, you know, but it *is* a women-only group.'

'No, I suppose he couldn't, could he?' Tamara had seemed struck by the novelty of being able to do something her father couldn't. Clare could see her mind ticking over behind the ruffled brow. Nagging her father for attention had backfired; perhaps she might get her revenge by shutting *him* out! 'But I'm so scrawny.' She looked down at herself with dislike. 'I'll look horrible in those clinging things.'

'Better than having rolls of fat bulging all over the place,' said Clare briskly. 'We'll just make sure we get you a fattening colour in horizontal stripes, the sort of thing which makes me look like an elephant.'

Tamara had produced her rare giggle, and Clare had thought what a nice girl she could be when she forgot to shoulder her chip. What she really needed were a few interests of her own. For all her sophistication, in some ways Tamara was less mature than Tim. She had told Clare that she had turned thirteen a few months ago, had shown her the gold locket on a chain that her father had given her, and talked about the party that Deverenko had arranged for her, long distance, since he was in Japan at the time.

Four days ago Clare might have condemned David Deverenko for abandoning his daughter on her special day, but having seen them together she conceded that he was having every bit as difficult a time of it as Tamara. He undoubtedly loved his daughter, but her prickliness and her unpredictable moods had him at a loss. They spent all day together while Tim was at school and Clare was concentrating on shutting out her intrusive awareness of the new presence at Moonlight in her work, and yet still Tamara wanted more. That made Deverenko impatient with her, which in turn made Tamara sulk. It seemed a vicious circle with no break in sight. To fully satisfy Tamara's demands Deverenko would have to give up his career, sacrifice his love of creating great music for love of his daughter, and if he did that he would not be Deverenko any more. That he realised it was obvious in the dark concern with which he watched his daughter when she was being particularly morose. That Tamara didn't was also obvious. If she did, Clare thought she would probably be horrified at the very idea, and yet that was what she wanted, to be first in her father's life—before his music. There would be even more pain ahead for the girl if she continued the self-destructive round of confrontation and selfish demand. Pain for David, too, watching the slow alienation. Clare's heart ached for both of them.

'Mum? Are you ready to tuck me up?'

'Just coming, Tim.' Clare went into his room and began their night-time ritual of discussing their day and planning the next one.

'Miss Tyson let Mr Deverenko take my lesson today.'

'Did she?'

'Then he played us a sonata on her violin. Did you know that he didn't bring his own down with him?'

'No, I didn't.'

'I wanted to see it. Did you know it was famous? I looked it up in a book. It's a Guarneri, they're even rarer than Strads, you know. Of course he has a Stradivarius, too, and a Tononi. You'd think he'd have brought *one* down with him,' Tim's piping voice was much aggrieved. He frowned. 'Unless he's going to leave soon. He couldn't not practise for more than a week, could he, Mum? Not Deverenko!' The thought obviously appalled him. From the first time his chubby toddler's hands had laid on the violin, Tim had played every day. It was unthinkable to spend a day without practising. In all the books he read, it was the the cardinal sin.

'He played today,' Clare pointed out.

'Not for very long. He practises at *least* four hours a day, longer than that, too, because of rests.'

'I'm sure he knows what he's doing,' placated Clare, wondering herself what it portended. She, too, found it difficult to think of David Deverenko without a violin within reach of his magic fingers. 'Perhaps his violins are too valuable to bring down here. No doubt the dampness and central heating wouldn't do them any good.'

'No, but you'd think he'd have brought an old one.'

'Why don't you ask him about it?' Clare said. Tim was like a terrier when on the track of a problem. 'How did your maths test go today at school?'

Tim decided it was time to snuggle down. He wriggled his small body down under the down cover and yawned impressively.

'Tim?' his mother said warningly, and he sighed, his brown eyes soulful, and so like Lee's that Clare weakened.

'It was boring, Mum. It was all stuff we've done already.'

'That's the idea of tests, Tim—to find out what you've learned. If Miss Tyson, or Mr Deverenko,' she added for good measure, 'didn't ask you to play the practice piece you've learned, how would you feel?'

'That's different. That's never boring.'

'Not even scales?'

Tim's mouth firmed stubbornly.

'I take it you didn't do too well in the test.'

'I didn't finish it. I got to thinking...' He tailed off as he watched his mother's face cloud over with hurt. He swallowed hard. 'I'm sorry, Mum, but I knew it all, really. It was baby stuff, long division and tables and things.'

'You should have done the test *first*, then done your "thinking",' said Clare firmly, with an inward sigh. She had already warned Tim's schoolteacher that he found the normal maths syllabus no challenge at all. Although Tim was a class ahead of his age group, he still found the work too easy, when he was sufficiently stimulated to tackle it!

'Never mind.' She leaned forward to kiss his smooth forehead, sprinkled with the freckles that adorned her own. 'I'll have a word with Mrs Campbell.'

'About book week, too? Why do all my reports have to be on those silly fiction books?'

'Because it'll do you good to read something imaginative rather than practical for a change.' This was something she *had* made progress with. 'Fiction is rather like music, Tim...one person's special vision of the world to be shared with others. They're all very well-written stories on the young adult level. I think you might find that you enjoy them.' And learn from them. One was about a gifted young pianist who had to face the fact he might not be able to play again after a car accident. She wanted Tim to realise that there were sometimes other obstacles than lack of talent or application that could get in the way of a burning desire to dedicate one's life to something. She feared for that fierce determination in one so young; it could so easily turn against him.

'OK, Mum.' Tim gave her the sweet smile that was his special gift. 'I love you, Mum.'

This was ritual, too. 'I love you, too, Tim. Sweet dreams.' She clicked off his bedside-lamp and went to the door.

'Mum?'

'Mmm?'

'Why can't we remember dreams?'

Clare smiled to herself in the darkness. Typical of Tim to end the day with a question.

'Our subconscious protecting itself, perhaps. Why don't you look it up in the library tomorrow?'

'OK.' Another yawn, but a real one this time.

Clare was still smiling as she closed his door and went to switch on her automatic kettle while she fetched her book from the bedroom. It was a thrilling spy novel, and Clare was looking forward to a little vicarious excitement. She switched off the main light in the lounge and put on the table-lamp next to the big, soft velvet sofa. She could hear the kettle beginning to steam, so she tucked the book under her arm and was getting out a cup for herself in the tiny kitchenette when there was a soft rap on the door. Clare sighed.

David Deverenko's eyebrows shot up when he saw her night attire. He was still wearing the white cashmere sweater and dark trousers he had worn at dinner. 'Going to bed already? Or are you expecting someone else?'

'Miles is still away.' The impact of him, leaning casually against the doorway, made her snappy defence instantaneous. 'Who else would I be expecting?'

'While sugar daddy's away... That photographer seems to hang around your office rather a lot.'

Her surprise was answer enough. 'Doug?' She was undecided whether to be annoyed or amused. Doug was gay. It was far more likely to be David he was interested in than Clare! 'You seem to have it fixed in your mind that I'm some kind of *femme fatale*,' she said in exasperation. 'I don't know where you get your ideas from, but you're way off beam.' What did he see when he looked at her, for goodness' sake? She was a twenty-seven-year-old mother, not particularly pretty or sexy, living a rather ordinary and unexciting life. 'And Miles is not my sugar daddy,' she was unable to resist adding.

'Do you sleep with him?'

'David!'

'Just want to make sure I'm not stepping on anyone's toes,' he said mildly, accepting her spluttering outrage as his answer.

'You might get your own crushed,' she warned him grimly.

'Only might?'

'Will, then,' she corrected herself, furious at letting him fluster her yet again. She should expect the unexpected from him by now. 'David, I'm tired. What do you want?'

His eyes gleamed, but he ignored the opening. 'A little company, that's all. Tamara's plugged into some unspeakable horror video——' Clare frowned at this, the freckles between her straight brows forming little ridges, and David sighed '—I checked the rating, little mother, it's OK for teenagers... it may be unspeakable to me, but then I'm a coward about these things. Tamara doesn't seem to find it particularly scary, and I don't think it will be detrimental to her mental health in the long run. I'm not a *totally* inept father, you know.'

'I never thought you were,' Clare said faintly, because it seemed to matter to him what she thought.

'Don't think I haven't felt your disapproving maternal eyes watching us,' he astounded her further by saying, his dark eyes suddenly very much like his daughter's when she was brooding on some slight, real or imagined. 'I can't be a father *and* mother to her; she remembers Nina far too well to accept my poor efforts as substitute. They were very close. Sometimes I think that her behaviour stems from the fact that she blames *me* for killing her mother. Nina was flying out to Rome to join me when the plane crashed.'

'Surely not——' Clare blurted reassuringly. Was that really what he thought? Or was he just voicing his own deep-felt guilt?

'Look, can I come in? I really don't feel comfortable talking about this in a corridor,' he asked ruefully.

She hesitated, fighting the automatic reflex to agree. Was this just a ploy to get in the door?

'I was just about to relax on the couch with a Russian spy,' she murmured, taking the book out from under her arm. Then she realised what she had said and blushed.

His eyebrows rose again. 'Won't a musician do?' he murmured with sensuous amusement.

'David...' They both heard the weakness in her voice, and he followed up his advantage.

'Please? A lonely musician? I'm far safer than a spy.'

'That's a matter of opinion,' said Clare, to his delight. 'I suppose you can come in,' she sighed, thinking that she must be mad to invite...whatever it was she was inviting. 'But just for a little while,' she warned, more for herself than for him.

'Just long enough to finish the bottle,' he promised, moving past her.

'What bottle?' Her eyes fell to the hands which had remained tucked behind him for the short duration of their conversation.

'This one.' He had two glasses, also, crystal flutes from the bar. The bottle was champagne, vintage Krug at over one hundred dollars a bottle, a filmy chill misting the green glass.

'We can't drink that.' Clare was used to the extravagance of guests, but her own economical soul balked at sharing it.

'I'll get drunk if I drink it alone,' he said, putting the glasses down on a coffee-table as she absently shut the door, and ripping the foil off the top of the champagne. 'You wouldn't like me when I'm drunk, Clare; I become very maudlin and depressed, very black-Russian.'

'You forget, I've seen you knock back the vodka. You couldn't get drunk in a month of Sundays,' said Clare wryly. David had brought the bottles with him, bearing incomprehensible labels in Cyrillic script, and instructed Kerry to keep them in the freezer.

'Vodka is an exuberant drink, company in itself. Champagne shouldn't be drunk alone, it has *tristesse* in its bubbles. Here, taste.' He handed her a brimming glass.

'I hope you put this on the spike,' Clare said to counteract the shivery thrill of the first sip.

'I do not need to steal for my pleasures, Clare,' he said quietly.

'I didn't mean... I was joking,' she said awkwardly. She had expected a flippant reply, not this stern dignity. She would never understand the man!

'So... enjoy. It's not a crime, Clare, to indulge in a little luxury... nor is it one to want to share it with friends.'

'No, of course not.' She felt terrible now, and she took a large, hasty gulp to make up for it. The bubbles exploded in the back of her throat with a heady burst of dryness that made her nose tingle, and she began to cough. David clicked his tongue and took the forgotten book and the glass from her, and put them down with his own glass on the table before he slapped her sharply between the shoulder-blades.

'Better?' he asked, as her coughs spluttered to a halt.

'Yes, thank you.' Her eyes were watering and she was sure her nose must be red. She must really look a sight.

'Here.' As if to confirm it, he held out a handkerchief and she took it to cover her embarrassment.

'Thanks.'

'Let's sit down, shall we?' He indicated the couch. 'For a novice like you, it might be best if you didn't have to worry about drinking and standing up at the same time.'

'I have had champagne before,' Clare told him tartly, as she returned his handkerchief.

'But not, judging from your horror, of this quality. Do you know how many dollars' worth you just wasted in that sneeze?'

It was as if he had read her mind. She glared at him, but the look was wasted. He was showing interest in her robe where the wrapover section had slipped with her choking breaths, his grin fading at the sight of pale lavender lace. He looked up and found her watching him, and there was a breathless moment when neither could look away. Clare was suddenly achingly conscious of her body. Because she had a slight allergy to man-made fibres, she couldn't wear anything but wool, cotton or

silk immediately next to her skin. As a result, her underwear and nightwear was all either extremely cheap and
prosaic or, like the lavender silk nightgown, sinfully
exotic and expensive. It was one of Miles's little gestures
of appreciation that each time he came back from
overseas he brought his valued Moonlight staff members
a gift. For Clare it was invariably underwear, usually
French, the kind she could never dream of affording
herself. Over two years, she had built up quite a
wardrobe, Miles turning a deaf ear to all blushes and
protests.

'I . . . I think I should go and get dressed,' said Clare
nervously, beginning to back away, feeling threatened by
the curiosity she could see in the dark eyes. He wanted
to see what the lace was attached to, and to her horror
Clare could feel her breasts tingling against their fine
silk covering.

'No!' The word jerked out, uncomfortably loud in
the small room. 'No, don't run away.' He smiled soothingly at her, his voice warm and encouraging as he picked
up her glass and handed it to her, resolutely keeping his
eyes away from her intriguing neckline. 'Just a few drinks
and a little conversation, Clare. Where's the harm in
that, mmm? Sit down. Don't be so tense. Nothing terrible is going to happen.'

That was debatable, Clare thought as she she numbly
obeyed. Something terrible had already happened. She
had *wanted* him to look at her. . . to touch her. She looked
blindly down into her glass. It hurt, this wanting. It was
wrong . . .

'Don't look so tragic, Clare. There's nothing wrong
with a man looking at a woman, or vice versa. It doesn't
have to lead to anything,' he said as he sat beside her,
and the hint of amusement stung. Clare lifted her chin.

'It won't.'

'Of course it won't. . . if you don't want it to.' He smiled
at her with a beguiling tenderness. It surprised her, this
gentleness in a man who looked so harsh and masculine.

'Now...what were we talking about before we were...distracted? Ah, yes, my daughter. Dare I suggest that I think you might be good for her? That damned school she was at seems to have had no idea how to control her.'

'Is that what you want? For her to be controlled?' asked Clare, relaxing fractionally now that the conversation was focused on *him*.

'I put that badly. Not controlled—*channelled*. She has much energy but no sense of focus, no ambition... beyond this fixation that she wants to look after me.'

'What's so awful about that? You're her father, the only family she has. It's natural she should want to be with you.'

'Actually I'm not—her only family, that is. Nina's parents are still alive. They live in Paris and they'd be happy to have Tamara live with them and go to day school there, but she rejected that idea, too. It's not just being with me she wants, Clare; she wants to do things that a wife does. She wants to be a replacement for Nina, and I can't let her do that—to herself or to me.'

'Oh?' Clare was lost. Surely he didn't mean...she moistened her suddenly dry mouth with champagne. No, not David, his instincts were very healthy...

'Why are you looking at me like that? As if I am from under a stone?' She blushed, and his eyes narrowed to black slits. 'Clare? Surely you don't imagine...?' He swore. It was in Russian but she was positive it was a swear word. *'Clare!'* For a moment she thought he was going to snatch back his champagne and storm out, then he threw back his dark shaggy head and began to laugh.

'For one who tries to be so controlled, you have a shockingly uncontrolled imagination,' he said, enjoying her discomfort.

Was that how she appeared to him? Controlled? Oh, thank goodness! thought Clare.

'I was not talking sexually, my prurient-minded madonna,' he reproved as he refilled her drained glass. 'I meant emotionally. It's not as if I require a replacement for Nina; that part of my life is now finished...' Did that mean he didn't intend to marry again? There certainly didn't seem to be room in his schedule for another wife. 'And certainly I don't want Tamara to be one of those people who sacrifice their own lives to the safety of living it vicariously through others, forming obsessive ties in the process.'

Clare stiffened. Was that a dig at her? She looked at him sharply, but he was staring out of the large picture window at the moonlit lake. All the rooms faced the lake, and on clear nights like tonight, with the moon full and heavy, a silver pathway opened across the still waters.

'Perhaps she doesn't see it as a sacrifice,' Clare pointed out gently. 'Perhaps she wants to do it out of love.'

'But that's what it would be. She would be Deverenko's daughter, not Tamara.'

'She's that already.'

'No, she's that *still*.' He looked up and caught her struggle to understand. He leaned forward, the dark fabric stretching across his broad thighs. 'Love and independence aren't incompatible, Clare. I want Tamara to discover that herself; I want her to finish her schooling, to have the experience of friendships and knowledge beyond the tight musical circle that encompasses *me*.'

'You can't force her into independence, not if you want to keep her love.'

He sighed. 'I know, but what can I do? We've tried tutors and companions. It worked while Nina was alive, because she made sure that Tamara respected them, but when I'm travelling and performing I don't have the time to give her the continuity of supervision that she received when we were a family unit. She ran rings around every woman I hired—and fired. So then we tried her grandparents—and now the school. Tamara has become an expert in lack of co-operation, in running away from situations she doesn't want to face. I fear for her, Clare, but I believe that if I give in to her manipulating I'll be creating a rod for both of our backs. Do you know she used to play the piano and violin? But since Nina died she has just refused to play any more. I won't say she had great talent, but she was a competent player——'

'Damned with faint praise,' murmured Clare.

His dark eyes were fierce. He tipped back his head and swallowed his champagne in one hard gulp, as if it were vodka. 'Damn you, I wasn't being condescending. I don't *care* whether she's a virtuoso or not. In fact, I was glad she didn't seem to care about a career in music—it's a hell of a struggle in the middle ranks—but music for *pleasure* . . . to play for *pleasure*, one's own pleasure . . . she knows how important that is to me. She wants to share in my life, yet she won't share this vital pleasure with *me*. I don't care if she never has another lesson—but to turn her back on it entirely, it wounds me.'

'Perhaps that's her intent.' Yes, to a man with music in his soul, it would be a powerful weapon to use against him.

'It probably is. That's also disturbing. I don't want her to gear her life to pleasing or displeasing me.'

'That's a father's fate, I'm afraid.'

'And a mother's?' he asked broodingly. 'Does Tim cause you to run around in circles?'

'Tim is different; he has his focus, as you do, and he's still very young. I know people who have teenage children and they invariably tell me that daughters are the most difficult—or perhaps it's just their sexist expectations, thinking that girls should be sweet and placid and obedient. Tamara has spirit, you should be glad of that, and she's of an age where most girls start to resist the authority of their mothers. Tamara's training her sights on the next best thing . . . you. As long as she knows that you love her and won't turn your back on her——'

'You mean I should give in to her?' he said sullenly. Obviously he was not happy with the direction of the conversation. Did he expect her to automatically side with him? Was that the way it usually went when he poured out his troubles into a willing female ear? Did they murmur, *'Oh, you poor darling,'* and fall into his hands like ripe plums?

'No, I mean never give up caring, being angry or stern, or autocratic, all the things that fathers are meant to be. As long as you resist *her* resistance, she'll know you care.'

'You're very wise.'

He wasn't being sarcastic. The brooding look had been replaced with a wry warmth that made her blush as if he had said something outrageous. She looked quickly away, sternly reminding herself of those ripe plums.

'Here I'm supposed to be learning about you and Tim, and all I've done is talk about myself,' he said softly. 'I'm sorry if I've been boring.'

'Don't be ridiculous,' she said, sure that he was teasing her. David? *Boring?* He had just given her a fascinating glimpse of the man behind the violin, the very human man. 'You're far more interesting than I am.'

'You think so?'

There was no mistaking the tenor of that murmur. Clare felt her skin heat up all over again, and she fiddled with her glass. 'Of course. You've done much more with your life than I have with mine.'

'What's that got to do with it? The most sophisticated people can also be the most boring. Look at the lake out there—it's quiet, unspoiled, with a natural beauty that makes one ache. It looks empty, but it's teeming with life at all levels. You could live a lifetime here and never know it all. I have the feeling that you're like the lake, Clare: you have a wealth of fascination under that beautifully still exterior. Is there fire beneath the ice, Clare? These beautiful lakes were created out of fire, weren't they?'

'I . . . I think you'd better go.' Clare set down her glass with a click, feeling unbearably flustered. Was he saying he thought she was beautiful and fascinating, after all the beautiful, fascinating women he must have known? She wouldn't let herself believe the lie.

'Why? Have I embarrassed you? By complimenting you? Why do you treat me so gracelessly? Didn't your husband teach you to accept compliments in the spirit in which they are offered? Didn't he tell you that you were beautiful?'

Clare couldn't bring herself to look at him in case he was laughing at her. Her hands were twisting in her lap. She felt as if she was on a train, rushing towards some unknown destination. 'Yes, but——'

'But what?' he asked, distracted by the new freckles revealed by her charming blush.

'But he wasn't . . . *flirting*.'

'He didn't flirt with you?' He frowned disapprovingly.

'Yes—no—you're confusing me,' she said feebly, wishing now that she still had her glass to fiddle with. 'Lee was my *husband*.'

'And you were a faithful wife?'

'Very,' she said firmly.

'And you still are?' There was a faint question mark at the end of his soft statement, but Clare ignored it. Certainly her thoughts of the last few days hadn't been very faithful to Lee's memory. She got up, suddenly stricken with guilt, but before she could suggest that he leave David changed tack.

'Virginia said that Lee played classical guitar. She said that he had a very bright career ahead of him.'

Clare half turned, so he wouldn't see the quiver of her mouth. She would bet all she had that Virginia hadn't mentioned the other side of the coin, her son's bright career in rock. 'Yes,' she said. 'Everyone agreed he had loads of talent. It's a pity he didn't record more than he did.'

'You mean he made a *record*?' David's surprise contained a faint suspicion he was being had. Clare looked too sweet and rosy and innocent and amused.

'He made several professional recordings. He wasn't famous by your standards, of course, but within New Zealand he was very well-known.'

'Then why haven't I heard of him? Did he record under another name?' She could see David sifting through his formidable memory.

'No, his own. In fact, I have one of his albums here. Would you like to hear a track?'

'I'd love to,' he said with enthusiasm. Not only would he be able to satisfy his curiosity about Clare's husband, but he would have an excuse to stay in the quiet intimacy of her company for a little longer.

Clare found the *Myth* album and put it on the turntable, making sure that David didn't get a glimpse of the cover. She adjusted the volume fairly high. The rooms at Moonlight were all insulated and fairly well sound-proofed, and Tim was a solid sleeper.

She wished she had a camera when the first thundering chords of the electric guitar vibrated around the lounge. David winced, shock, dismay and finally comprehension streaking across his dark features. Clare was openly laughing at him when he rose slowly to his feet.

'*This* is your husband?'

The vocals started and Clare turned the volume down slightly as she nodded, her eyes limpid blue. 'What's the matter, don't you like it?' She was fairly sure of his answer, and was therefore stunned when he tilted his head and listened for a moment to the strong, husky voice doing the vocals and the clever, catchy rhythm that threaded behind it, beginning to click his fingers and move to the beat.

'It's good. I like it.' And as if that entirely settled the matter he moved towards her, still in rhythm, shoulders and hips gliding sinuously in time. 'Dance with me.'

'We can't,' said Clare automatically, dragging her eyes away from the intriguing tilt of his pelvis.

'Why not? There's nobody to see us.' He danced around like the Pied Piper, forcing her to turn to keep him safely in sight. 'Doesn't the music make you want to move? That's the hallmark of good rock, it makes you want to illustrate the beat. Come on, Clare,' he invited mockingly, 'you know it's irresistible...'

And it was. She was already swaying without realising it. 'This is ridiculous,' she whispered as she let him loosely clasp her wrist and draw her across the lounge to the empty space in front of the big windows. He was a marvellous mover and she couldn't help but respond, her own love of dancing overtaking her, challenging her to better him. Soon they were embarking on an absorbing interaction that banished her self-consciousness. She wasn't even aware that one track had melted into another, until David's hands were at her waist and she realised that they had reached the slow number, the last one on that side. They had been dancing for twenty minutes. When she tried to ease out of his grip he wouldn't let her. He held her wary eyes with his, drawing her into their dark fascination, beckoning her with the tantalising brush of his body.

'We move well together, don't we?' he murmured smokily, his hands on her waist turning her so that her hip moved against his, one of his thighs briefly pressing between her legs. He turned her again before she could protest the intimacy...if she had wanted to. They danced in silence a few moments longer, then the eyes which held her captive dropped to her mouth. Clare became exquisitely conscious of his body, the arousal that he teased her with every time he moved against her. Yet perversely she didn't feel threatened. Yes, he was aroused and not trying to hide it, but explicit in the dark admiration of his eyes was the promise of seduction, not rape. His body, though taut with desire, was relaxed, asking rather than demanding.

'David...' she began shakily, trying to find the strength of will to deny the unspoken question.

'Do you like the taste of my name in your mouth?' he whispered, eyes dark slits as he watched her lips move.

She wanted to taste more than his name, and he knew it. Clare shivered, pressing herself inadvertently against him, and he gave a soft groan.

'Yes, darling... move like that... again... Clare...' One hand was now binding her waist, the other sliding up into her thick, clean hair. 'Mmm, you smell so good...' He continued his erotic dance as he kissed her, enjoying the faint quiver of her mouth before it opened obediently to the gentle thrust of his tongue, accepting the inevitable. She filled his senses, her warm, womanly curves fitting to him, making him arch to relieve the ache that was threatening to explode. It wasn't enough. He broke the kiss slowly and with the greatest of reluctance, his fingers tightening in her hair as he looked down at her upturned face, flushed with the heat of mutual desire. Her eyes were the colour of a stormy sky, her mouth as lush and ripe as the rest of her, faintly swollen by his quest for the pleasure within. Had he bitten her in his delirium? He lifted his hand from her waist to trace the over-full bow.

'You have a lovely mouth.' It seemed natural to let his hand sink down again, over the delicate arch of her jaw, down her soft, warm throat to the creamy, freckled triangle of skin above the modest embrace of her robe. Clare's eyes fluttered closed, shutting out the hunger that hardened the aggressive angles of his face. She mustn't see... she mustn't let *him* see, know, how much she wanted to appease that very male hunger.

He knew what she was doing. 'Don't hide from me, Clare. You don't have to hide yourself from me.' He kissed her again, and from somewhere Clare found the sense to stiffen the arms she had braced against the hard wall of his chest. Even so, her tongue curled treacherously around his as she dragged her mouth away, as if she couldn't bear to let go of the sinful delight of the symbolic possession.

'No, please...' She couldn't seem to breathe very well, the roomy robe seemed too tight. 'David...'

'It's all right, it's all right, Clare,' he soothed her trembling with tender kisses along her averted jawline, his fingers abandoning their tormenting of that tender triangle of skin as they moved instead to the tie of her robe. 'It's all right. I'm going to go. I just want to see what you're hiding. I won't hurt or frighten you...'

He wouldn't, but Clare frightened herself. She wanted him to see her body, even though she was afraid he would find it disappointing. She looked at his face, dark and intent, as he slowly unwrapped her robe, deliberately prolonging the agonising moment of anticipation.

His hand clenched on the soft lapel of the robe as he stared at the lavender drift of pure silk which faithfully loved every dip and curve of her body from breast to knee. The lace bodice cupped her breasts with exquisite restraint, the transparencies in the pattern providing tantalising glimpses of creamy flesh bearing its own random pattern of freckles. The tight points were modestly covered, but that only made them all the more obvious.

Clare waited for him to touch her, to slide the silk against her heated skin, her abandonment complete as she saw not disappointment but the flattery of raw desire in his silent appreciation.

He sighed, the hard body seeming to arch slightly towards her yearningly before he shook his shaggy head and firmly rewrapped her robe, tying it more tightly than was necessary.

Clare went pale, then hot with shame. She had practically melted into his arms, and he didn't want her. He had been just flirting. Probably he was amused that she was so easy, after all! She tried to pull away, but he wouldn't let her.

'Clare, do you know what the time is?'

'*What?*'

'Tamara's movie will be over. And if I know her, she's not going to sit quietly in our room until I come back. She's going to come looking for me.'

'Oh?' Clare's eyes shot everywhere but to his face, and he gave her a little, sharp shake.

'Clare, I'd love nothing better than to make love to you in that lavender piece of nothing, but even now you're having trouble looking me in the eye. Imagine how it would be tomorrow morning, if I stayed and did what we both want. I came here to talk, not to seduce you. The seduction comes later.'

'Oh, really? You mean you have a schedule you have to stick to?' said Clare, infuriated enough by his arrogance to glare directly at him.

'No. But I think you do. I don't think that you're the kind of woman to sleep with a man on the first date.'

'This wasn't a date!'

'Even worse!' He looked shocked, and she very nearly succumbed to his teasing. Just in time, she stopped the smile.

'David——'

'Let it go, Clare. You really don't want to pursue this.' And suddenly she didn't. He looked all too confident of where it would lead. She wished she had the kind of sophistication that could shrug off what just happened.

'Now, show me nicely to the door and give me a consoling goodnight kiss, and bear in mind when you wake up next morning that I've been incredibly self-sacrificing!'

Smug wretch! He didn't get his kiss, but it didn't seem to bother him. Clare could hear him chuckling all the way back down the hall to his room.

She went over and switched off the stereo, offering a silent apology to Lee's photograph on the back of the album cover.

If only Lee were here to protect her now. The trouble was that he wasn't, and she couldn't help remembering one of the last things he'd said to her, in the hospital, when he knew there was not much time left.

'Life is for living, Clare, you just remember that. You've gotta take your chances as they come. If you don't, you're only *half* living!'

CHAPTER SIX

'HELLO, Tamara, have you seen Grace? She's not in the kitchen.' Clare didn't really hold out much hope of a positive answer from the figure scrunched in the huge, over-stuffed chair by the french windows in the spacious lounge. Tamara ignored people and things that she didn't like, and Grace was not in her good books. The cook's habit of responding in kind to surliness and bad manners was an unpleasant shock for someone who was used to more satisfying reactions of outrage and anger.

'No.' Tamara was frowning morosely at a layout of stunning models in one of the glossy fashion magazines that she had brought back from her last trip to Rotorua. Clare felt a tug of empathy. She, too, had mourned over the world's unreasonable expectations of feminine beauty when she was an adolescent—tall enough to be a model, but not thin or pretty enough. Temporarily abandoning her quest for the dinner menu, she wandered over to where Tamara sat and was about to make some wry comment about air-brushed fantasies when her eye was caught by a burst of activity down on the lake shore.

'What's going on down there?' David and Tim were jumping about on the grassy slope bounded by lake, lodge and bush, flapping their arms loosely, the small, sticklike figure of her son an absurd contrast to the solid, muscular man in a white polo-necked sweater and black jacket and jeans.

'I don't know,' said Tamara with airy indifference, not looking up and thereby revealing that she was very well aware of the two males outside. Had she been hoping that her father would look back up to the lodge and feel guilty at the lonely silhouette in the window, or was she

95

really trying to follow Clare's advice at the gym, and struggling to assert her independence?

Clare nibbled her lip. 'Tim is supposed to be practising his violin. It's his sacred after-school ritual. I'm surprised that even your father could lure him away from it.'

'Dad doesn't have to lure. He just *is*,' his daughter said with a mixture of childish pride and adult resignation. Then she cast a sly look at Clare. 'People usually end up giving him what he wants. Especially women. It's embarrassing how far some of them will go to try and please him. But in the end he just pleases himself. You'll see... if he really wants to take Tim away to his school, he will... and have you helping him do it.'

Take Tim away. The words echoed in Clare's mind, as no doubt Tamara intended them to. When Tamara had discovered that her father had spent part of the evening two nights ago in Clare's suite, she had reverted to open animosity, until she had noticed that, far from improving the acquaintanceship, whatever had passed between them had stalled it. It had taken Clare a long time to get to sleep that night, and her dreams had been so full of forbidden music that she had been relieved to wake up the next morning. Her vulnerability had appalled her. She had behaved like the proverbial sex-starved widow. Thank goodness he had not taken advantage of her momentary weakness—although, far from being grateful to him, she was outraged. His self-control made her lack of it all the more humiliating. And he had the gall to suggest that her falling into bed with him was a foregone conclusion!

On the other hand, he hadn't renewed his attempted seduction since. On the contrary, he made no attempt to be alone with her or be anything but passingly friendly. That raised Clare's hackles, too. Either he was confident that she would eventually come begging for his attention, or he had had some deeper, darker motive for treating her like a desirable woman. Like Tim. He might not be able to take Tim away from her physically, but there were other ways to loosen the tie between mother and son. Could she trust David, as a confused parent himself, not to use a subtle form of propaganda to pressure Tim's young, impressionable mind into rejecting her parental authority? Or should she trust that other instinct—fear—which warned her to run like hell?

'Well, you may not be interested, but I am. Coming?' Clare opened the french doors and stepped outside, her shoulders set determinedly.

'No, thanks,' said Tamara, content with having stirred the pot. Now her father's playful idyll with the interloper would be broken up and Tamara hadn't even had to lift a finger. She could afford to feel virtuous.

Down at the lakeside, man and boy continued to imitate the birds who winged gracefully above the cold, still waters. As Clare neared their capering she could see Tim's face aglow, his breath whitening the cold afternoon air. He looked quite warm in his down jacket and jeans, but his hair and his sneakers were damp, and she could hear the faint rattle in his throat.

In spite of her determination to be casual, she was aware of the faint bite in her tone as she said, 'I think it might be a good idea if you came inside now, Tim. You know you're supposed to do your homework before you come out to play.'

'But I'm not playing. I'm practising!' He looked surprised at his mother's sharpness, and she couldn't blame him. Usually she was pleased to see him enjoying himself in the fresh air.

'For what? Flying?' Clare refused to look at David, preferring to pretend she wasn't aware of him with every nerve cell in her body.

'David is showing me some relaxation exercises. He always does them before he plays. He told me to call him David,' he added quickly as he saw his mother frown at the familiarity.

To her annoyance, David moved up beside the boy and put a casual arm across the thin shoulders, as though protecting him. 'Usually I'm called plain Deverenko by my students, but I didn't think that would fit in with Tim's description of your notions of propriety.'

He made her sound like a prig, but politeness was essential when one lived in a hotel. Clare looked at him, her eyes as cool as the mist beginning to form on the lake behind them. 'Besides which, Tim is *not* one of your students,' she pointed out succinctly.

He inclined his head in silent amusement at her tartness, and the word *yet* vibrated silently between them, causing the tension in Clare's stomach to coil tighter. He looked uncompromisingly masculine in the soft black leather jacket, with a dark shadow of re-growth on the hard jaw and a glitter of challenge in the dark gaze. His eyes flickered down over Clare's simple grey tailored dress with its flared skirt, cuffed collar and long sleeves. It was very demure, and the white lace bra and briefs she wore underneath were equally demure, so why did she suddenly feel sexy from the skin out? Unconsciously Clare pressed a nervous hand to her chest, and when David's eyebrows rose she snatched it away, angry at the defensiveness the gesture had revealed.

'Well, I think you've done enough for today,' Clare redirected her wayward thoughts to her small son. 'It's getting pretty cold and damp out here and I don't want you catching a cold. Run in and get out of those damp clothes, and I'll get you a hot drink from the kitchen. Then you can settle down to your homework.'

'But I haven't done my practice piece yet. David is going through it with me. He was just showing me how to breathe and loosen up my muscles. And I'm not cold, really I'm not. Feel.'

Tim thrust one warm little hand into hers.

'Perhaps not, but you will be as soon as you stop moving. At least get out of those damp shoes and towel your hair before you get out your violin.'

'OK, Mum.' Tim was eager to obey now that he had proved his point. With a beseeching look at David to hurry, he scampered off towards the lodge.

'You can't keep him wrapped in cotton wool forever, Clare,' David murmured as she turned to follow. 'If you coddle the boy too much, he'll never stand on his own two feet... if that's what you want.'

Clare whipped around, hands on hips, all too ready to argue. 'I don't consider taking reasonable precautions with his health "coddling". Since he was ill last year, Tim has been very susceptible to infections. Couldn't you hear him wheezing? And if he's in poor health he can hardly take a serious interest in the violin, can he, considering the endurance and fitness it requires?'

'I'm sorry, I didn't know he'd been ill. Does he suffer from asthma?' David asked quietly, defusing her anger somewhat.

Clare nodded. 'Not badly, but enough to complicate common chest infections. For a while after Lee died he used to get regular attacks, but I think they were more psychological than physical. He used to worry that he was going to stop breathing when he went to sleep. Lee lapsed into unconsciousness before he died, and although Tim read all about leukaemia and seemed to understand, I think he became overly aware of his own physiology.' She smiled faintly. 'The curse of a very active imagination.'

'Better to have too much than too little. It is getting a little chilly out here. We were so engrossed, I didn't notice. I have a great tolerance for it... my arctic Russian blood, I suppose.'

'I thought Russians were hot-blooded,' slipped out involuntarily, and Clare began walking, hoping the small exertion would excuse her flush.

'It depends on the circumstances,' he said with a grin as he fell in beside her.

'Do you consider yourself Russian rather than a New Zealander?' asked Clare steadily. 'I notice your publicity always calls you a 'New Zealand-born Russian.'

'That's Efrem's psychology. He claims everyone expects the best musicians to have Russian ancestry, and being born here removes the taint of communism that US audiences find suspicious. I have been to Russia—once—during a brief thaw in the political ice-wall. You know my parents were refugees? Well, my father continued to be an active, vocal critic of Russian politics right up until the day he died...particularly as it involved the repression of creative free-thinking in the arts. He was considered a traitor, and I, as the son of a traitor, was only issued a visa under sufferance. I was visiting my mother's only sister who was dying, exchanging messages. I have no doubt I was kept under surveillance, and I wasn't allowed to perform, but even so I felt a certain sense of homecoming. Perhaps, with the advent of *glasnost*, I may be able to play there one day. I'd certainly like to see more of the people and the country, but I'm a child of democracy, of freedom, and the illusion of homecoming was just that, an illusion, prompted no doubt by all the nostalgic tales my parents and their friends fed me. There's nothing more Russian than an expatriate Russian, even a dissenting one.'

'So where is home?'

'Physically, nowhere. I have properties in London and New York where I spend so much time, but I usually prefer staying in hotels, so that I don't have to be concerned with domestic details. Emotionally, it must be here, at the school. I have a house in the grounds and that's where I live when I'm not performing, so I suppose you could call that my *home*. Certainly it is my link between past and future, my gift, if you like, to this country for offering my parents refuge and safe citizenship. We Deverenkos like to repay our debts.'

'But you didn't really live here very long, did you? I mean, you went to America when you were still quite young.'

'To learn to become a musician, not to learn to become an American. It is the first blissful memories of childhood that always grip us most. I like the climate here, I like the gentle pace of life, the peace, the safety that comes from belonging to a small, isolated country far distant from the embattled turmoil of the superpowers. I shall retire here when I am old and grey, and surround myself with the new generation of musicians to sustain me in my decline,' he announced whimsically.

'I can't imagine you in a decline.' The thought made Clare's rare, sweet smile surface. 'More likely you'll grow more arrogant and demanding than ever as an *éminence grise* worshipped by all those young, unquestioning minds.'

He laughed. 'If you think that young musicians worship blindly at the altar of experience, you have a sad awakening ahead of you. Young musicians are every bit as arrogant and opinionated as old ones, once they have a little learning under their belts. That is the danger. When I was in my late teens I was sure that I knew better than all my teachers, I thought I could do anything and the critics seemed to agree with me. But while I enjoyed the temptations of the high life, basking in all the adulation I was receiving, my playing suffered. In anyone else the flaws might not have been remarked upon, but the standards by which the critics judged me were, after all, my own... or had been. Music was my life, but it had chosen *me*... how could I betray the honour? So I came back here and shut myself away for a while and re-learned the lesson of humility: there is no music without discipline and dedication. One plays a piece, but one *thinks* it also. That was the beginning of my maturity, I think, both as an artist and as a man. Shortly afterwards, when I rejoined the concert circuit, I met Nina and the maturing process was completed. She, too, had a serious sense of vocation and understood the pressures that drove me. Loving Nina provided me with emotional depths that until then I had lacked. That had been the only suggestion of criticism—that my playing was too cold, too perfect. Mastery of your instrument is not enough, you see...a brilliant technique is an empty vessel if it contains no subtle nuances to tease the listener, to provide the musical revelation.'

Fascinated by the dreamy seriousness of his expression, Clare stumbled over a rough piece of ground and might have fallen if David hadn't whipped out a hand and steadied her. He saw the look in her smoke-grey eyes and made a sound in the back of his throat.

'Ah, Clare, don't look at me like that.'

'Like what?' She blinked, removing the arm around her waist so that she could walk on. In spite of the explosive speed with which he had moved, the hand which had caught her had been gentle, unsettlingly so. Aggressive vitality and gentleness; it was a potent combination.

'As if I am some alien species that you don't know whether to fear or trust—or care to do either.'

'But you are...an alien species, I mean,' said Clare, shaken that he should read her so well. 'I can't even begin to understand you or your world.' She sighed with relief as they gained the stone steps.

'Why don't you come and sit in on this practice with Tim? Perhaps that will help dispel some of the mystery.'

'I...' For some reason the offer disturbed her even more than his touch. 'I have the menu to type.'

'It will only take half an hour of your time. You can give Tim that, can't you?'

It was very cunning of him. Her eyes flashed. 'I can give *Tim* all the time he needs.'

'Good.' He smoothly steered her past her office towards the small room, with piano, that Tim used to practise in when there were no guests to disturb.

'I...Cheryl doesn't believe that parents should interfere with a child's practice,' she protested weakly as David sat her in a chair and turned to Tim, who had sorted out his written assignment from his music case and was rubbing rosin into his bow.

'You're not going to interfere, you're going to appreciate. I agree that critical judgement from a parent can be counter-productive, but as a source of moral support there's no substitute for a mother's smile.'

'I'm glad you agree I have *some* uses,' Clare murmured drily.

David swung around on the piano stool and gave her a sensuous smile that made her regret her unwary words, but he didn't say anything, allowing her own thoughts to put her to blush and laughing softly when she obliged. After his restraint of the last day or so, his teasing warmth had double the impact. She realised suddenly how much she had missed it, even as she had told herself that she was grateful for the respite.

Watching David break down his art into its basic components for her son was indeed a revelation for Clare. For all the vast gap in age and experience, there was a mutual respect between the two that allowed them to communicate as equals. David made no attempt to impose his own highly individualistic style on Tim. When the boy made mistakes, David didn't take over to demonstrate the right way, *his* way, of doing things, but instead urged Tim to discover for himself how and why he had gone wrong. He was teaching Tim to listen outside himself, to trust his own ear and vision of how the music should be interpreted.

The two serious, absorbed faces, so unalike and yet so similar in that hungry quest for perfection, sent a pang through Clare's breast. She had lost him, she realised, that loving little boy who had nestled against her heart. He didn't need her nearly as much as her maternal jealousy had insisted that he did. Oh, he loved her and clung to her love because he knew it demanded

nothing of him, but he was already reaching out for
something else, the kind of stimulation and challenge
that her efforts to cushion him from further hurt had
denied him. She had striven so hard to create a sense of
'normality' for him, to make up for the loss of his father
and his feelings of alienation. But Tim was *not* normal,
and never would be. Perhaps only someone as special
as David was could truly show him where he fitted in,
could guide him to fulfilment.

She felt exhausted by her inner turmoil by the end of
the intense session. A tiny voice of protest questioned
her sudden about-face. Was it David Deverenko's personal magnetism that was swaying her, or reasoned
judgement? Tim was still the same boy he had been a
week ago when she had still been rock-certain of the
wisdom of her guardianship, so was it Clare who had
changed? David not only had her doubting her worth
as a mother, but also re-evaluating herself as a woman
whose feelings hadn't been buried with her husband.
Moonlight, which had been a haven and home for
eighteen months, was now taking on the inexorable shape
of a trap with David Deverenko as the tasty, tempting
morsel of cheese! If she took the bait, what then?
What—or who—did he *really* want? And could she face
it if it wasn't her? If she continued to reject his professional advice about Tim, would he disappear from
her life as suddenly as he had appeared?

'Well, do you approve of my methods?' David murmured quietly as Tim packed away his violin after doing
a few wind-down exercises. 'Perhaps I'm not the whip-
cracking autocrat you expected me to be, mmm? It is
Tim who sets the pace, not the teacher. A good teacher
merely responds and guides. A good teacher also knows
when a student has outstripped her.'

Clare stood up jerkily. 'Are you talking about Cheryl?'

'She admits it herself.'

'Then why hasn't she said anything to me?'

'She was unsure how to approach you. She knows how protective you are of the boy, and she knows that you have no desire to move away from Moonlight. That rather limits the options, wouldn't you say?'

Clare's fists clenched with the effort of restraining her temper, all too conscious of Tim's presence. Her voice was low and defensive. 'I suppose I've no need to ask which option *you* favour? After all, that's why you're here, isn't it?'

'It was certainly the reason I came,' he admitted, his murmur an octave below hers as he moved closer. The warmth of the central heating suddenly seemed stifling as his broad shoulders blocked out Clare's view of Tim, making her feel isolated, the sole focus of all that masculine warmth. 'But now I'm here, I'm discovering another, equally compelling reason to stay...'

Clare took a breathless step back, and his dark eyes narrowed with predatory satisfaction as he caught her hand and carried it to his lips to caress it silkily with his breath.

'I'm not normally a patient man, Clare, but I made an exception in your case. It looks as if that was a mistake. You're very adept at avoiding reality. I think you've become spoiled in this little peaceful niche of yours. Well, this time reality has come to *you*, and I won't let you hide from it.'

'What are you kissing Mum's hand for?' Tim came up alongside them before Clare could pull her hand away.

David didn't take his eyes off her. 'Because your mother's too shy to let me kiss her on the mouth.'

'You want to kiss her?' Tim frowned at him. 'Are you in love?' He turned the possibility over doubtfully in his mind.

Clare's eyes sparkled defiantly. Let him get out of *that* one! Her hands flexed helplessly in his steady grasp. David didn't seem in the least embarrassed by the question.

'I don't know. I find your mother very attractive. Men and women kiss each other for a number of reasons, Tim; love is only one of them. A kiss can be a very serious expression of affection, or it can be for fun.'

Tim wrinkled his nose. 'Who'd want to kiss girls for *fun*?' He sounded so disgusted that even Clare had to smile. David chuckled, relaxing his vigilance enough so that she could at last slip her hand from his.

'It's a purely adult concept of fun. I'm sure you'll learn to appreciate it as you mature.'

'You're talking about sex.' To Clare's further amusement, David actually pinkened as his condescension rebounded on him.

'I take it your mother's taught you about the birds and the bees,' he said when he had recovered from his momentary speechlessness.

Tim looked at him in askance. 'That's not about sex. Birds and bees can't mate—they're two different species. Only two of the same species can produce babies. That's how I was born. My——'

'Er—yes.' David cut Tim off before he could air the extent of his precocious knowledge, casting a darkling glance at Clare's suspiciously straight face that promised revenge. There was no stopping Tim once he was determined to home in on a subject of interest, and his curiosity about where babies come from had stemmed from the birth of some puppies that he had witnessed. Clare's edited lecture about sex had not been enough for Tim. He had insisted on knowing all the details which, once absorbed, had provided the basis for a school project about the origin of the species. To Tim, sex was just one tiny cog in a far greater diagram of the machinery of life on earth. 'I think we're straying off the subject here a bit, Tim,' David chose his words more carefully this time. 'What I'm trying to say is that I would like your mother and I to be friends, and to do that I need to get to know her as a person. How would you feel if she and I ate out tomorrow night?'

'Outside? In winter? Isn't it a bit cold and dark?' Tim looked dubiously out the window.

His instant literal interpretation of David's words was very revealing. David hid the satisfied gleam in his hooded eyes as he explained to Tim the alien concept of dating. 'No, I meant that I want to take your mother out to a restaurant in Rotorua, just the two of us.'

Clare opened her mouth, but Tim beat her to it. 'Why?'

'To...talk.'

'About me?'

'You'll probably come into the conversation some-where,' said David wryly, acknowledging the innocent self-absorption.

'Then why can't I come?' Clare relaxed slightly as she recognised the stubborn expression on Tim's narrow face. She wouldn't have to refuse, Tim would do it for her.

'Because I want to be alone with your mother. Don't you think it's important that your mother and I be friends?' Tim considered that for a moment, then nodded. 'Well, in some ways the beginning of a friendship is like learning to play the violin. It needs some devoted concentration and privacy to develop properly, before one exposes it to the stresses of public performance.'

'Oh.' Illumination was complete. Tim's stubborn look became the pride of martyrdom. 'Well, I suppose you have to go by yourselves, then.'

'Wait a minute! Don't *I* have some say in this little arrangement?' cried Clare, betrayed by her own flesh and blood.

David and Tim looked at each other, one of those irritating man-to-boy looks, then David frowned and turned his head from side to side in bewilderment. 'Who said that?' Tim giggled.

'I might have a previous engagement,' said Clare coolly.

'And pigs might waterski,' replied David, confident of his ground. Tim's giggles intensified.

'Time you were in the bath, young man,' Clare told the traitor sternly and, egged on by his ally, Tim saluted.

'Yes, ma'am. But you will be friends with David, won't you?' he hesitated long enough to ask.

'I——'

'Of course she will. She's only pretending to be reluctant,' said David smoothly.

Tim trotted off, violin case tucked under his arm, reassured, while Clare was left to hiss fiercely, 'Do you usually have to resort to using innocent children to get dates?'

'Only when their mothers make a habit of hiding behind them,' he said silkily. 'You want to come, Clare, you just *think* you shouldn't. So I helped relieve you of the burden of the only reasonable excuse to deny yourself. Now you can pretend you're doing it just to keep Tim happy.'

'Of course, it's beyond the bounds of possibility that a woman could actually refuse David Deverenko.'

'Not "a woman". You. Why the song and dance, Clare? Are you afraid you might enjoy yourself, after all? Would that be so unnatural? You're an attractive, mature, single woman. Why shouldn't you enjoy male companionship once in a while? It would be unnatural if you *didn't*...'

She wasn't unnatural, just cautious, Clare told herself the next night as she got ready for her first 'date' in over seven years. If it had been any other man she would have accepted or refused the invitation according the impulse of a moment without ruffling a hair, but with David her impulses were inclined to lead her dangerously astray. They made her wish for the forbidden—to be young and free again, untrammelled by responsibilities, unshadowed by the past. If she didn't have Tim to anchor her heart and her life, she might have tossed her cap over the windmill and thrown herself into the kind of wild, passionate, fleeting affair that David offered.

She looked at herself gravely in the mirror, sobered by the thought. She didn't see the beauty of the wide grey eyes, or the sensuality of the rosebud mouth, or the charm of her creamy, freckled skin and honeyed waves. She saw a loving mother who for a guilty moment wanted to deny her motherhood, deny the son who had given her life meaning. How could she, even in fantasy, wish that he didn't exist? What kind of monster was she? Or was it something all women faced, the opposing pull between the fulfilment of a biological and emotional drive and the desire to be free, like a man, to roam, to hunt, to live life on one's own terms?

Clare adjusted the ruffles on her cream silk blouse and smoothed her black velvet skirt. The gold band on her left hand was her only adornment—Lee hadn't been able to afford an engagement ring, and it hadn't mattered, for their love was the only jewel Clare had coveted. She thought she looked just right, feminine but not flirty, attractive but in an austere, monochromic fashion that she hoped would reaffirm her intention to remain aloof from any attempt at seduction. Yet she couldn't help the quicksilver trickle of exhilaration through her veins at the risk she was taking. Clare, who never took risks! David would view her aloofness as a challenge. He would look at her with that dark, exciting glow in his eyes and seek to break down her reticence...

She heard Tim call out, and curbed the wicked trend of her thoughts as she went into his room. By rights he should be well asleep by now, but as soon as she saw him Clare's heart sank. Her mouth tautened as she ran to his side, disgusted with herself for her momentary twinge of impatience. Tim was leaning against his pillows, struggling for each harsh breath. Clare helped him sit up, talked soothingly as she straightened his back and tried to encourage the rest of his body to relax.

'Try and breathe from your diaphragm, Tim,' she urged, putting her hand against the lower part of his chest as with her other hand she fished in his bedside drawer for his inhaler. Usually his breathing soon eased, but tonight the air still whistled through his restricted air passages and suddenly he leant over and retched, vomiting all over the bedclothes and Clare's skirt. The spasm seemed to unlock the muscles in his throat, but soon his rasping breaths were clogged by sobs. Clare whisked the soiled bedclothes back and held his shivering body against her for a few minutes until his crying settled to a series of dull shudders. Murmuring a reassurance, Clare slipped into the bathroom to sponge off her skirt and fetched a warm, soapy flannel and towel so that she could clean Tim up. She undressed him, put on fresh pyjamas and held his head over a bowl as he retched miserably again. When she was sure that he had finished being ill, she got the sheets and duvet from her own bed and tucked it around Tim, brushing the damp hair off his pale forehead.

'Better now?'

Tim nodded, but tears squeezed out of the corners of his eyes. His silent misery thickened Clare's own throat. She knew that, even if Tim felt well enough for her to leave him, she couldn't go out now. She would spend all evening wondering how he was.

'Breathe deep and slow.'

'My tummy hurts.'

'I know, darling; you squeezed all the muscles when you were sick.'

'My throat's burning, too.'

She got him a little boiled water from the kettle and he drank it gratefully. His breathing was still irregular, but at least he didn't bring up the water.

'Are you going soon?' Tim quavered, his hands tight on the sheet.

'I think I'll stay home tonight. I can go out another time,' Clare told him lightly.

'Will David be angry at me?'

'Of course not, honey, he'll understand.'

'But you won't be friends.'

'Of course we will. Now, you just snuggle down while I get rid of these sheets. Shall I leave the light on?'

Tim nodded wanly. 'You wouldn't go without telling me?'

'You know I wouldn't, Tim. Now you close your eyes and relax the way the doctor told you. If you need anything I'll be just here in the lounge, OK?'

'OK.'

Clare dialled David's suite as soon as she had delivered the sheets down the hall to the laundry, and fetched new ones, leaving her door open in case Tim should decide to test her honesty.

Tamara answered with laconic disinterest.

''Lo?'

'Tamara, it's Clare. Can I speak to your father?'

'He's just getting ready for his hot date.'

In her agitated state, the sarcasm passed Clare by. Besides, she had already put up with countless little digs, between puffs, during a workout in the gym that afternoon. She had been surprised, given Tamara's outrage at the learning of the dinner *à deux*, that the girl had deigned to join her, but the reason was soon obvious. Water dripping on stone had nothing on Tamara. Clare had been given chapter and verse of all the brilliant, talented, witty, rich, gorgeous women who had set their lustful sights on her father.

'He might have slept with them, but he didn't care about them; he just moved on to the next woman in the next city. He's not looking for permanency. He's had a vasectomy, you know, so he doesn't have to worry about being trapped by a woman with an eye to the main chance. My mother had a really tough time having me, and the doctor warned her not to have any more children. Dad loved her enough to sacrifice any future hope of sons to carry on the family name. That's probably why he's paying so much attention to Tim. Tim's just the kind of son he'd like to have had.'

'I really don't think you should be telling me this, Tamara,' said Clare tersely.

'Why not? You should know what you're in for if you're planning an affair with Dad.'

'I'm not planning anything. It's just a simple dinner,' Clare lied. Nothing about her feelings for David Deverenko was simple.

'Sure.' The single word was loaded with scepticism. The fact that it was partly justified drove Clare into working particularly hard at the routines, and she felt a mean sense of satisfaction when Tamara's competitive hostility insisted that she keep up with the pace. Sweat dripped off the tense young face, and Clare couldn't help but be impressed by her dogged persistence and the fluidity of her moves after an initially jerky start.

'I hope you haven't overdone it,' said Clare, feeling guilty as the girl stumbled on their way back to the changing-rooms. Tamara looked very young and vulnerable, all angles in her colourful leotard. 'I shouldn't have pushed you so hard.'

'Why did you, then?' Tamara demanded, expecting some adult prevarication in response.

Clare smiled ruefully to herself. 'Revenge, I guess. I wanted to pay you back for telling me some unpalatable truths that I'd rather have ignored.'

Tamara was struck into silence for a moment before she, too, smiled half-heartedly. 'Hey, who's the juvenile around here, you or me?'

Clare accepted the weak joke in the spirit it was offered. 'It can't be me, I feel at least ninety.' She sat down on a bench and rubbed a calf muscle. 'I think I'm the one who overdid it, trying to keep one step ahead of you.'

Tamara slumped on the bench beside her, mirroring her exhaustion. 'I feel pretty wobbly myself,' she admitted frankly. 'It's a lot harder than it looks. But you know what? Although I feel shattered, I feel good!'

She looked so surprised that Clare laughed. 'That's the idea. And the great thing about "jazzercise" is that once you have the moves and a music tape, you have your own portable gym. It's fun to make up your own routines and invent new variations on old ones. Do you want to come again?'

Tamara was instantly diffident. 'Maybe.' But a few minutes later she was preening when the instructor passed them in the foyer and said, 'You're new, aren't you? You were pretty good for a beginner. You were really reaching for it and you have a good sense of rhythm. You'd better look out, Clare, or this protégé of yours is going to have you eating dust!' The last comment had pleased the girl no end.

Now she ignored the girl's sarcasm, and said, 'Tamara, I need to talk to your father.'

'Why?' She could tell the girl was enjoying keeping her dangling.

'Because Tim is sick.'

'You mean you're not going out, after all?' Tamara sounded elated by the news. 'Just a moment, I'll go and tell Dad——'

'Tamara——' Clare winced as she imagined how the girl would phrase the news, but the receiver had already thumped down.

Then there was a clatter as it was picked up again, and she was surprised to hear Tamara say, 'He's not really bad, is he? The kid? I mean, he seemed pretty OK this afternoon.'

She and Tim had actually spent some time together playing a video game on the office computer, a cartoon-character one that made losing as interesting as winning, and involved typing in instructions rather than merely working a joystick or firing button. They had treated each other with casualness bordering on disdain, but there had been surprisingly little open conflict. Now

Tamara sounded as if she was bothered that 'the kid', as she enjoyed calling him disparagingly, might be seriously ill.

'No, I think he's just got a chill, but I don't want to leave him. Tim gets a bit worked up about illness, which only makes him feel worse, and he hates being left alone.' Shari had promised to come and babysit, but Clare knew from experience that when he was in the grip of one of his unreasonable terrors Tim could be pacified by no one but his mother.

'Just hang on, I'll get Dad.'

'Clare?' From the hollow echo and the faint sound of water running, she realised that he must be using the cordless phone in Miles's bathroom.

'David, I'm sorry but——'

'Just a moment. Tamara, you can hang up now.'

There was a snort and a click, and some of the echo was reduced. 'Now, Clare, what is it? Cold feet at the last minute?'

'No! Didn't Tamara tell you?'

'That you're still hiding behind Tim? Yes. I'm not as gullible as my daughter, Clare. If you don't want to go out with me, you can damned well tell me honestly to my face.'

'But——'

He had hung up on her. Clare fumed. If he thought she was *that* much of a craven coward, why did he want to go out with her? Damn the man for his arrogance. Naturally he would assume that *he* was at the centre of every situation!

A few moments later she had the chance to vent her anger to his face when there was a sharp knock at the door.

David was in no better mood than she. His pale shirt was hastily buttoned, a fleck of shaving cream on his chin indicating a hasty wipe.

'Well?' he growled at her, folding his arms across his chest. His eyes flickered over her, taking in the make-up veiling her freckles and her subdued finery. 'All dressed up and nowhere you dare to go?'

Clare glared her affront. 'It may be common in the circles *you* move in to put your own selfish enjoyment above the needs of others, but not in mine. My son is sick and he needs me. And I would far rather disappoint your arrogant expectations than his!'

'Where is he?'

'In his room, and you are not going in there looking like a thu dercloud.' She barred his way, bristling with outrage. 'He's already worried that you'll be angry with him, and I won't have him more upset.'

'Are you sure he's not just putting it on?'

'Yes, I'm sure,' Clare gritted. 'Now, will you please leave?'

There was a stiff moment of silence. 'I'm sorry. I guess I thought you might try to cry off, and I was pre-programmed to shoot my mouth off. Can I see Tim? Just to reassure him that there are no hard feelings?'

Smiling suavely, he edged around her and Clare let him go. Let him see for himself that she was telling the truth.

Tim's breathing was harsh in the quiet room, and his face pale except for two hectic red spots high on his cheeks. His eyes looked huge in his small face, sad and watery, and his young mouth was suspiciously stiff. He would hate to cry in front of his hero.

'Hello, old son, having a tough time of it?' David's voice was soft and musical, no hint of his former temper.

Tim nodded, afraid to unlock his brave lips.

'Never mind.' A square hand cupped the boy's tight chin. 'You take it easy, and if you're still feeling bad tomorrow I'll play for you for a change. How's that? Deal?'

Tim nodded again. 'But you haven't got any of your violins,' he managed waveringly.

'That's because they're having a rest. Violins, es-pecially the best old ones, are like people—they need to be rested every now and then. And I just happen to be one of those lucky ones who can take a break from playing and pick it up again without ill effect.' He smiled. 'I discovered that when I was ill once myself. I fretted and fretted about not practising, but when I came to play again I found myself much more relaxed and open to the music. So now I make sure that at least once a year I have two or three weeks in retreat. That's what I'm doing now. But for you I break fast. I can use your violin.'

Tim smiled wanly. 'It's too small.'

'For these magic fingers?' David waggled them comically. 'You wait and see.'

'Thank you,' said Clare softly when they were back in her lounge.

'For not making a fool of myself? Anyone can see that he's not well,' said David abruptly. 'Have you called a doctor?'

Clare shook her head. 'I've given him some of his asthma medication, but this is really only a mild attack. Maybe he's got a cold coming on, or has a flu bug—his resistance isn't very good to that type of thing—and then he began to panic when he felt sick. I told you about Lee . . . I wasn't at the hospital when he died, and Tim knows that and so he likes to know I'm around when he's ill. I guess in a way he *is* putting it on, but it's something that he has no control over, and in this case it doesn't pay to be cruel to be kind. I've tried it, and that's when he gets his severest attacks.'

'It's all right, Clare, you don't have to convince me. I feel guilty enough as it is,' said David, cutting across her anxiety. Clare looked very like her son with her pale, earnest face and tense determination not to give in to her fears. Her mind was wholly with Tim, he realised ruefully. David was just a distraction that she didn't really want or need. She had coped before on her own, and that was the way she preferred it. The feeling of thwarted protectiveness, of helplessness, reminded David of the way his daughter made him feel. He was well aware that she viewed his interest in the Malcolms with dismay. Perhaps tonight might be a good time to try some tentative fence-mending. Tamara had all but ignored him for the last few days...perhaps she was waiting for her father to make the first move...

'I'll leave you to look after Tim,' he said reluctantly, turning Clare towards him with a firm hand on her shoulders as she frowned towards the bedroom. 'But let me say first that you look very beautiful, and I'm sorry that the evening has to end before it's begun.' He had her attention now, and he savoured her gentle blush at the sensuous promise in his eyes. 'Another time, perhaps?'

'Perhaps...' Clare murmured vaguely, wondering at the swift succession of emotions he evoked in her. He had made her feel guilt, anger, tenderness and desire, all in the space of ten minutes. Somehow he bypassed her reserve and pierced to the passionate heart of her. His eyes flared with need at her dreamy response, and it was only as he drew her into his chest that reality impinged on her hypnotised state. A faintly sour smell clung to her evening skirt, and reminded her of her obligations.

'Not even a consolation prize?' murmured David, not understanding why she pushed him away, but resigned to the total annihilation to his hopes for the evening.

'I...Tim was sick on my skirt. I haven't had time to change it yet,' said Clare, grabbing the velvet folds against her in embarrassment.

'And you think that might put me off?' David guessed. 'My darling girl, I'm far less squeamish than you seem to think. I've dealt with my fair share of dirty nappies and upset stomachs. Nina made sure I kept in touch with the flip side of parenthood.' He reached for her again, but she backed away, the mention of his wife reminding Clare of all the women that he had romanced—most of them probably just as gorgeous as Tamara had claimed they were. None of *them* would have glided into his embrace smelling of 'eau de sickroom'. She wanted to be their equal, not pitied and equated with memories of unpleasant bodily functions!

David sighed. 'All right, Clare, have it your way. I'll call later and see how Tim is. If he gets worse or you need anything, you know where to find me.'

CHAPTER SEVEN

TIM had two more bouts of sickness before he finally fell into a fitful sleep around eleven o'clock. By that time Clare, who had substituted practical jeans for her ruined skirt, was feeling a few stomach pangs herself. She was hungry. The restaurant that David had booked into was one with a reputation for the very rich, heavy, classical French cuisine that Grace disdained, so Clare had prepared herself by eating only a snack lunch. Perhaps some food would lift her out of her depression—a mingling of disappointment and relief. Tim had probably done her a favour by falling ill and saving her from her own unruly desires.

She was debating whether it was safe to leave him for a few minutes and go and forage in the kitchen, or whether she should ring and see if Grace was still up, when the phone rang beneath her hovering hand.

'Is he asleep?'

David. His earlier phone call to check on Tim had been brief enough to cause her to feel slighted, as if he were impatient to have it over and done with so that he could abandon her to her tiresome maternal duties, so consequently Clare was cool.

'Yes.'

'Good.'

Clare listened in disbelief to the terminating click. So much for his appreciation of the flip side of parenthood. Suddenly Clare was both ravenous and angry. He could have at least asked how *she* was feeling!

Her mind made up, she pulled open her door and stepped into the hall, only to run into David, who was wheeling a covered trolley.

'Hungry?'

'I . . . yes.'

'I thought you might be. Hold your door for me, would you?'

Clare did so automatically, watching him wheel the trolley into her room and begin to lift off covers. When she didn't move, he paused with raised eyebrows. 'What's the matter?'

She opened her mouth to throw his generosity in his teeth, and then closed it again. That would be cutting off her nose to spite her face, the kind of thing that Tamara seemed to specialise in.

'I . . . I just wasn't expecting . . .' She spread her hands vaguely.

'You thought I would cheerfully go to sleep, perhaps even arrange for my appetite to be satisfied, with never a thought for yours?' From his silky tone of voice, Clare wondered which particular appetite he was referring to, and she flushed at both the implication and the accuracy in his sarcasm. 'I really am an utterly selfish bastard, aren't I, Clare? Never a thought of anyone else but myself. Heavens, I'm amazed I actually possess any friends, the thoughtless way I carry on . . .'

'All right, all right, I'm sorry,' Clare burst out as she pushed the door closed with her back. 'What do you want me to do? Go down on my hands and knees?'

He smiled at her, eyes heavy lidded as he looked over the incongruous combination of her best silk blouse and the tight jeans encasing long, shapely legs. 'The idea has a certain appeal,' he murmured huskily. 'There are things you could do for me on your hands and knees that I find myself wanting very much . . .'

Clare went from pink to scarlet. Even the most flirtatious guests she had fended off had never resorted to such explicit suggestion. She looked anywhere but into the now laughing dark eyes.

'Calm down, Clare, I was only teasing. My motives are . . . were . . .' he corrected himself with amusement, 'pure as the driven snow. I knew you'd be feeling wrung

out, so I asked Grace to put something together for us.'
He looked ruefully down at the laden trolley. 'She told
me it served us right for trying to sneak out to "that
artsy-tartsy French joint". This spread is her idea of
rubbing it in.' He began to lift silver lids. 'We have crab
timbales, cold babaco soup, venison, strawberry and cu-
cumber salad, and little fruit tarts with whipped cream.'

'I think I'm going to faint,' groaned Clare, drawn like
a magnet towards the delicious fragrances mingling above
the warmed salvers. David had included a bottle of wine,
and even two candlesticks, which he placed on the small
table in the corner of the room, where she and Tim ate
on the infrequent occasions that Clare cooked for them
on the small range in her kitchenette. She fetched cut-
lery and napkins from the dresser drawer while David
dished up. Far from a romantic, candlelight conversation, they were both so absorbed in the food that they
hardly spoke until they had finished the main course.

'Feeling better?' David asked, his face half shadowed
in the soft light.

'Yes, thank you,' said Clare meekly as she enjoyed
the rich, full flavour of the Australian red wine he had
chosen. She finished her glass and held it out for some
more.

'Are you sure? On top of the night you've had, it might
just finish you off.'

Clare had never pouted in her life, but she did so now.
She felt full of warm contentment, a lazy sense of well-
being that she wanted to sustain for as long as possible.
'I'm not a child, David. I can hold my liquor.'

'I'll drink to that,' he said drily, and poured her half
a glass before finishing off the bottle himself. 'Why don't
we sit by the fire to eat these tarts?'

Although the lodge was centrally heated, all the suites
and public rooms had fireplaces that were kept burning,
often day and night during the winter, not only to con-
serve the heat draw-off from the bore, but to provide
the atmosphere that Miles wanted to engender.

'I couldn't eat another thing, but you go ahead,' said Clare, taking her half-glass of wine and sinking on to the wide, thick sheepskin which covered the floor in front of the stone fireplace. She wouldn't have bothered lighting it herself, but Shari had come in and done it for her, saying that since Clare was probably going to have a late night ministering to Tim, she might find the fire companionable. Actually, she had. Too restless and anxious to read, she had found sitting down staring into the flames very soothing.

David put three or four of the small tarts on a plate and joined her. He ate two and then licked his fingers. Clare smiled.

'What's funny?'

'Magic fingers.' She reminded him of the phrase he had used to Tim.

'And so they are. Would you like a personal demonstration?' He swivelled around until their faces were level, lying on his side, his body propped on his elbow as she leant back on her hands. He, too, had changed since their earlier encounter. He had on a black V-necked cashmere sweater that looked even softer than the sheepskin beneath her palms, and it had slid over on one shoulder, showing a strong ripple of muscle and a thick mat of hair on his chest—dark, like his head, with flecks of grey.

Clare swallowed. 'No, thank you . . . I told you I could hold my liquor,' she added smugly, when it appeared that she was safe, he wasn't going to lunge.

'You said you weren't a child, too. But when you smile like that . . .' He lifted a finger and touched her cheek very lightly. 'You dimple like a chubby baby, all sweet powdered innocence.'

For some reason that offended her, and she latched on to the only acceptable line of objection. 'I'm not chubby. Thin people can have dimples too, you know.'

'Mmm, but you're not thin.' He grinned. 'You're just chubby where it counts. And you have the most fantastic legs I have ever seen...like fluid muscle sheathed in cream satin, smooth and hard. What a waste to hide them in trousers.'

Instead of bristling at his chauvinism, Clare's inner warmth increased. She turned on her side to pick up her glass, taking the opportunity to ease back a few discreet inches, so that her leg no longer brushed his. 'I don't usually,' she admitted. 'I much prefer wearing skirts, but when you have a son, jeans are sometimes handy to have around...particularly when his digestion's uncertain!'

'It was the first thing I noticed about you.' David wasn't really listening. The finger that had explored her dimple was now tracing the outer seam of her jeans where it curved over her very unbaby-like hip. 'Your legs, wrapped around that ageing spiv.'

'I don't think Ray would appreciate being called either ageing or a spiv.'

David ignored her second attempt to deflect him. 'I couldn't help imagining you gripping me like that, holding me between your thighs. It excited me to picture you like that. And then you stung me out of my erotic fantasies by dismissing me like some slimy foot-in-the-door salesman. I planned right then and there that you weren't going to get away with it. Of course, I told myself that it was for Tim's sake, but all through my tour I had dreams about your lovely strong legs...'

She was staring at him, wide-eyed, little lights from the fire dancing in the grey depths, and he smiled. 'Do I sound like a fetishist? I never was before, but then you make me feel all sorts of things I never felt before.'

'Like what?' Clare whispered, trembling on the verge of discovery. She felt his hand slide back and forth along her thigh.

'Like the agony of self-denial. Here we are, having an intimate conversation in front of a roaring fire, filled with food, wine and desire, and yet I can't make love to you.'

Clare's eyes widened further still. 'W...why not?'

His hand tightened on her hip. 'While you're vulnerable with worry over Tim? While you're a little drunk and a lot weary? When your son may interrupt us at any moment? That's not what I want.'

'What do you want?' Clare asked huskily.

'That's the hell of it—I don't know.' He drank, recklessly, then discarded his glass on the hearth, not taking his eyes off her flushed arousal. 'Yes, I do. I want to see what you're wearing under those clothes. Ever since I saw that lacy thing you wear to bed, I've ached to know what other sexy secrets your cool modesty conceals.'

Clare's recklessness matched his. Her fingers went to the pearl buttons on the loose blouse and she undid them, slowly, one by one. David froze, scarcely breathing, as though afraid that any overt response would send her fleeing back to common sense. His restraint was justified. Clare couldn't really believe that it was her behaving so wantonly, so out of character, actually *teasing* a man with her body. The fact that he had said they couldn't make love only increased her excitement, made it safe to be wanton...

What she wore tonight had rather shocked her when she had first seen it, but since Miles had presented it to her she had seen similar garments appear on the racks of even chainstore lingerie departments, although of much inferior quality. And the fact that it was plain white had made her feel less wicked. It was a basque, with a row of tiny hooks up the back that it had taken a while to master, very flattering in the way that it scooped her breasts and followed the sweep of her waist to a saucy little frill on the hips. Clare didn't take her blouse off completely, she wasn't that bold, and when she had pulled the tail of her blouse out of her jeans and unbuttoned the last pearl she stopped. Her hands were beginning to shake too much anyway, from the sweet, hot darkness of David's eyes.

She moistened her dry lips, unnerved by his silence, and was bewildered when David suddenly rolled away with a groan, presenting her with a broad dark back.

'David? What's the matter?' For a moment she thought that he was ill. She scooted over to kneel in front of him uncertainly. 'David?' She bent to try and see his face, almost buried in the sheepskin, bracing a hand on the curve of his waist. He jumped as if he had been shot, and groaned again when he rolled on to his back and saw her bent over him, the creamy curve of her breasts pressing dangerously against the fragile barrier of French lace.

'Oh, Clare, you're killing me.' His hands moved up stiffly, as if against his will, to cup her shoulders under the loose sleeves of her blouse, thumbs moving over the soft skin as he dragged her down towards him. 'I promised myself I wasn't going to touch you. Why didn't you refuse me?' he demanded thickly.

Clare's breasts pinkened under his agonised admiration. A quick, sweeping glance over his body, and she had tingled with the knowledge of how much he wanted her. Now desire threatened to overwhelm his self-conscious nobility, and she didn't know whether to be scared or glad.

'I wanted it, too,' she admitted breathlessly.

'You shouldn't,' he told her, watching helplessly as his hands moved down to the glossy satin curve of her breasts, tracing the lucky freckles that kissed her creamy skin to their hiding-place in her generous cleavage. Her breasts seemed to rise against his fingers, trapping them in their shadowed valley. 'You know what I am, what my life is like. Are you prepared to let me do this in the knowledge of all our differences? Knowing that I can't possibly be comfortably slotted into your secure little world?' His eyes rose to hers, narrowing. 'Or is that precisely *why* you're inviting me to make love to you? Because you *know* I won't be here in a week? Are you just looking for a passing prince to reawaken your sexuality, someone who won't cause complications afterwards?'

Oh, if only he knew! She wanted to say, I'm doing this because I love you and I want you to love me in the only way you can. But she couldn't say that. Although his ego might be bruised at thinking of himself as just a passing phase in her life, it was better than him knowing the truth. The worldly, sophisticated musician had already known the one and only great love of his life, now immortalised in memory. No living woman could ever match up to that perfect memory, and he wasn't looking. He would run a mile if she said the words, so naïve, so demanding. To tell someone that you loved them in the knowledge that that love wasn't returned was little short of blackmail. Clare must bear that burden herself. It was no fault of David's. His had been seduction, pure and simple, no hiding behind false promises or vague hints of a possible future together.

'Clare?' David's face had darkened as he watched her mental retreat. His hands slid from her breasts to tightly encompass her waist. 'I won't be used just to satisfy your sexual curiosity. I don't want to be compared to your sainted Lee...'

Clare tossed her head, the movement making her breasts sway provocatively above her lightly boned waist. 'And I don't want to be compared with your Nina...'

'I would never do that. I told you, my marriage is over, gone. I've had other women since Nina, but I never made the mistake of comparing them, or even *wanting* them to be like my wife. Whereas you...' The gaze which roamed hungrily over her captive body suddenly contained an element of sullenness, as if her provocative appearance no longer pleased him. 'You haven't relinquished the past either physically or mentally. You've preserved yourself, held back all the passion in your nature except where it's safely channelled into the living shrine of your son, afraid of any real flesh and blood man who might crack that cool little shell of mourning...'

Clare tugged at the tensile strength of his hands, her mood of languorous enchantment dispelled by his piercing darts so near the truth. She *had* changed since the tragedy, had been afraid of new places and experiences after the upheaval of moving to Moonlight. The people who passed through its doors were mere acquaintances, too caught up in the adventure of the place, in their own luxurious lives, to press to enter hers. David had changed that, had changed *her* ... and that he had such power frightened her.

'I suppose you would have preferred me to have spent my period of mourning flinging myself at every man who came along,' she snapped, wriggling a lot and achieving little except a heightening awareness of the solid thigh flexing against her hip. 'I suppose if I'd racked up all the experience with casual sex that *you've* had, you'd consider that the key to re-entering the land of the living. Well, I'm sorry to be so provincial and middle class about it. But I loved Lee and I'm proud of it! And I never will look on sex as the only path to happiness and fulfilment, or something to be indulged in lightly or casually—and take your damned hands off me!' She was panting by the time she finished, infuriated by the way he was smiling as he watched the riveting metamorphosis from sultry, pouting sensuousness to doubt, to spitting fury. He had never seen her so uninhibited, and wondered what she would look like utterly so. Her eyes drilled into him like shafts of steel, her honey hair flaunting about her head, her cheeks rosy and the lush little bow of her mouth looking ripe to bite him. Her breasts heaved, and he could feel the intriguing flex of her diaphragm against his thumbs pressing her lower ribs. How in the hell could mortal man resist her? Why *should* he resist her? Even as he tempted himself, he knew the answer. All the reasons he had given her earlier were still valid. He wanted their lovemaking to be a leisurely voyage of discovery, not a quick, heated coupling that would cause a woman of conservative values like Clare agonies of conscience afterwards...the first time, anyway. His own conscience would offer no stumbling-block, whatever happened. He had known from the first what he wanted and was supremely confident of getting it, albeit with a little more difficulty than he had anticipated. But that would make the victory that much the sweeter...

'I don't account promiscuity a virtue, either,' he said smoothly. 'I haven't been with *that* many women, Clare, and I wasn't trying to malign your chastity. I just find it rather daunting, that's all.'

'Daunting?' Clare stopped pulling at his impervious hands and stared at him suspiciously.

He held her eyes steadily. 'Making love is something you consider very special, so special that only one man has touched you, seen you, though many men must have wanted to. That makes your expectations greater, not less, than a woman of experience. Your lover would have to be special, too—gentle and slow and very sensitive to your needs and responses, willing to withhold his own pleasure until you were lost in yours. He would have to be careful not to rush you, frighten you with his strangeness. He would have to make sure you were in the right frame of mind, and willing, not just for the moment, but for the next and next, for all the tentative little steps on the path to ecstasy. I would like to be that man for you, Clare.' He smiled crookedly. 'The flesh is willing, but the mind is weak. What if I can't make you feel the way you think you should feel? I'm not a man who takes failure lightly. It would shatter me to discover that I had disappointed you...it makes me almost afraid to try...and it makes me as defensively callous as an adolescent...'

Clare's bones had turned to water at his skilful verbal seduction, but the last, rueful show of weakness was a trace humble for a man of David's arrogance. Clare looked down into his innocent face, and lowered her lashes so that he couldn't see her expression.

'I wouldn't tell you.'

'What?' Expecting a passionate reassurance after the imperceptible softening of her body in his hands, David was taken aback by her cryptic utterance.

Her lashes lifted, her eyes gravely in earnest. 'If you were a disappointing lover. I wouldn't be so brutal to your ego. I would fake it. I'd lie and tell you that you were wonderful.' Her brow suddenly crinkled into a freckled ridge, and a hand came up to cover her rounded mouth. 'Oh! I suppose I've ruined it now. You'll never know what kind of lover you are. You'll always wonder if I'm only *pretending* to enjoy it. Oh, David, how awful for you!'

His jaw had dropped before he caught on. There was a stunned moment of silence, and then a wild flurry of movement as he dragged her down on top of him and rolled to pin her beneath him growling in half-angry amusement. 'Damn you, little tease, you've been begging for this.'

His kiss should have sent her into seventh heaven, but she was laughing too hard. He gave up after a while and lifted his mouth to glare at her sternly.

'Stop laughing, woman!' With a nudge, he shifted his jean-clad hips between her thighs, but to his chagrin Clare continued to laugh, although a little more breathlessly than before. 'Brutal to my ego? Clare, around you a man doesn't dare *have* an ego.'

'You should have seen your face,' giggled Clare remorselessly. 'You looked so horrified. Haven't you ever wondered before whether the lady was *really* enjoying herself, or just trying to please you?'

He grinned wolfishly. 'With me, they're one and the same thing. I'm glad this little joke of yours has sorted one thing out.'

'What's that?' Clare was now relaxed, at ease with the big body on hers.

'That we *are* going to be lovers. You said that I'll wonder whether you're pretending. You won't be, Clare,

because with me you're going to be completely uninhibited and utterly honest...'

'I...I was only teasing,' she said, flustered into
sobriety.

He smiled. 'I like it when you tease me with your
tongue. Do it some more,' he invited in a vibrating purr
against her mouth. This time his kiss had the desired
effect. Drowning in his sweet taste, Clare slid her arms
up his back, under the soft caress of cashmere. His skin
was hot and dry to the touch, a contrast to the moist
silk of his mouth. She had to explore his chest, too, to
see if the thick growth of hair was as soft and springy
as it looked. It was, and Clare slid her fingers through
it as David moaned encouragement, his flat nipples rising
against her palms. His mouth hardened, as she slanted
her head back over his arm so that her back arched and
he could feel the tension quivering through her body.
His mouth moved down her exposed throat to where the
silk blouse was thrown back from her shoulders. Here
he lingered in anticipation, the muscles of his chest rip-
pling beneath her hands as he supported his upper body
on his elbows. His head dipped and he kissed a slow line
across the taut flesh rising from the basque. The kisses
were followed by an equally slow string of erotic bites,
and then by kisses again as he murmured to her in
Russian. She didn't know what he was saying, but the
verbal stroking aroused her almost as much as the exquisite touch of his mouth. His thighs pressed against
hers, parting them, the two layers of denim an offence
to both of them. David's free hand slid against the
sheepskin to seek the low back of the basque. He ran a
fingernail down the long line of little hooks—and
groaned.

'Hooks...hundreds of them,' he despaired thickly.
'This damned erotic piece of underwear is a chastity
belt!' He punished her with another bite on her breast,
this one hard enough to sting and make her cry out involuntarily. He soothed it immediately with his tongue,

suckling the place until she cried out in another kind of pain—his kind—the pain of frustration. His hand moved to the dome of her jeans. 'Clare——?'

A faint cry came from the bedroom. Then another, louder. David swore in two languages, continuing to hold her down for a moment. 'Dammit. You see? I *told* you this would happen.'

'David——' It was a sigh and a plea. He knew there was no contest and wasn't about to argue. He shoved himself to his feet, his knee wedging briefly, with shattering deliberation, hard against the secret woman's heart of her as he did so.

'Go, dammit, *go*!' he ordered, backing away on stiff legs when it seemed she hesitated, fighting both her own desire and his.

The cry became a shrill scream of terror, and Clare's body was doused in an icy chill of dread. She and David made it to Tim's bedside simultaneously, the boy was sitting bolt upright, screaming and clawing at his throat, his eyes wide open and unseeing.

'What is it? Another asthma attack?'

'A nightmare.' Clare sat on the bed and took Tim's petrified shoulders in her hands and began to shake him gently. 'Wake up, darling, it's only a dream. Tim? Wake up! Mummy's here, Tim. You're at home in bed, *your* bed.'

'Heavens, does he have this kind of thing often?' David asked, appalled.

Clare was concentrating on waking Tim as gently and quickly as she could. 'Not as much as he used to. He dreams of being buried alive, of being trapped somewhere and not being able to breathe...often in a hospital bed. I told you, his father's death worried him.'

'But I didn't realise it was to this extent.' Tim was awake now, shivering uncontrollably, and he began to cry. He didn't even hear or see David, only his mother holding him safe and tight, helping him to breathe. 'Has he been counselled, seen a psychologist?'

Clare stiffened, alert to the implied criticism. Did he think she was such a poor mother that she wouldn't seek professional help when it was needed?

'I think you'd better go. It'll take a while to settle him down again.'

David drew his own conclusions from her stubborn evasion. 'Perhaps I can help——'

'No!' Already she was beginning to feel appalled at what she had almost allowed to happen, on the *floor*, for goodness' sake! It was *David* who had worried about Tim; she hadn't spared one thought for her son, she had been too deeply in the grip of conscienceless passion. She tempered the violence of her objection with a placating gesture. 'I mean, I don't think Tim would like to have you seeing him like this. He has his pride too, you know.'

'Perhaps you allow him too much pride. But then, you have an awful lot of it yourself, don't you? You have to do everything yourself in case people should see you as a less than perfect mother.'

She turned her face down to her son. David was so quick to sense her areas of vulnerability that she felt defenceless. 'Please, can we talk about this another time?'

David's mouth twisted wryly, feeling all the ground he had made during the evening slipping away beneath his feet. 'All right, Clare, but we *will* talk. I'll see you in the morning.'

Tim's pyjamas were drenched with sweat, so Clare changed them and gave him a drink of water before she tucked him back in. He was slightly feverish but, not surprisingly in view of his exhaustion, he lay down without a murmur and closed his eyes. Clare sat, stroking his head for a few minutes, and then frowned as she heard sounds in the lounge. Evidently David hadn't left, after all. For an instant she felt a rush of gratitude. She longed to go out there and fling herself at him, sob out her real feelings on his broad shoulder and trust him to make everything right with her world. But common sense prevailed. She must make him see that tonight had been a regrettable mistake.

She was into the lounge before she realised that the sounds were a conversation. To her horror, Tamara, her face flushed and mutinous, was standing by the half-open door, and it was obvious from David's taut expression and low, controlled voice that they were having an argument.

Tamara saw Clare first. Her eyes widened in shock, swiftly followed by a black contempt that struck Clare like a blow. Clare clutched at the edges of her blouse. She had been so absorbed in Tim and her guilty thoughts that she had forgotten to rebutton it. She quickly remedied the omission, but it was too late. Tamara had seen the white lace basque and the damning evidence of reddening on the creamy pale skin. She knew exactly what Clare and her father had been doing. Tim wandering out would have been bad enough, but Tamara, chock-full of more adolescent conflicts than she could cope with, was even worse. Knowing that her father had lovers was quite different from coming face to face with the emotional reality of a woman who, even if only briefly, had usurped her beloved mother's place.

'I...I thought you had gone,' Clare said faintly to David.

'Don't get dressed on my account,' said Tamara cuttingly, glaring in disgust at the swollen mouth that Clare couldn't possibly hide. 'I've been ordered back to my room so you can carry on with your——'

'Tamara!' It was the first time Clare had heard that musical voice crack.

'I suppose you're going to try and tell me that you were playing cards,' Tamara sneered defiantly. 'What were you playing? Strip poker?'

'That's enough, Tamara.'

'I'll say it is! You know, I was really beginning to think that you might be a friend,' she flung at Clare's tongue-tied humiliation, 'but you were only being nice to me so that you could crawl into my father's bed without me making a fuss.'

'Well, she certainly failed on that score, didn't she?' said David with a bitter sarcasm that offended both woman and girl.

Clare found her tongue at last. 'Tamara, that's not true. I——'

'You were pretending to like me and pretending to hate Dad, and I nearly fell for it,' the girl charged on, completely ignoring her father. 'Well, you can stick your stupid gym and you can stick your bloody two-faced friendship and your creepy son——' The genuine agony behind the fury made Clare's heart weep for her, but David was made of sterner stuff.

'All right, Tamara, you've made your point,' he said icily. 'Now, I suggest you go back to our suite before you make a greater fool of yourself. I won't have you insulting Clare, or insulting me by presuming to make judgements about an adult situation you know nothing about.'

'Oh, right. It's nothing to do with me, right?' Tamara yelled at him. 'Why should it be? I'm only your *daughter*. Your boring, stupid, ugly, talentless daughter who you can't even stand to have around! Well, that's fine, because I can't stand being around you, either. Why should I care, if you don't?' She turned her fury back on to Clare, although her words lashed out at her father. 'You think he cares about you, either? He'll dump you just like he dumped all the others, like he dumped me. So you better just enjoy the celebrity screw while it lasts——' She might have said something else, even more crude, but she glimpsed the building tidal wave of her father's rage out of the corner of her eye and broke off to flee, slamming the door behind her. There were no tears, but Clare didn't doubt there would be floods of them when she got back to her room.

'I'm sorry, Clare——' David began tightly. 'She woke and saw the time, and thought Tim might be worse.

When she saw the dinner things, she started acting like a betrayed wife. Hell, what a mess...' He ran a hand through the hair that only a short time ago Clare had ruffled in the freedom of desire. 'I knew that Tamara could be a vicious-tongued cat, but——'

'She's hurt and cornered, and feels the only way out is to fight,' Clare defended tiredly. 'Don't be too hard on her.'

David's anger slipped a cog. Tamara was temporarily out of his reach, but Clare was a standing target. 'And you're too damned soft! You'd have me let her get away with murder. You won't listen to the slightest criticism of *your* family relationship, and yet you're quite free in criticising mine. What the hell makes you such an expert? You have problems of your own that you can't solve, though it may please you to believe you have all the answers.'

'I never said that——'

'No? You think this nightmare problem of Tim's is just a phase? After two *years*? You don't think that there's something suspiciously manipulating in these timely asthma attacks of his? Your son is an extremely clever child. What do you think all this "there, there, Mummy will make it better" stuff is teaching him? That only you *can* make it better! That he can't rely on anyone else. You treat the symptom, not the illness, because you're too pig-headed to seek out the proper advice. I admit it—all right?—I admit it! Tim *wouldn't* be happy at the Music School, because there he would be just one of many with very special talents. Here he can be a genius. You think that by making him battle on here you're doing him a favour. You're not. Here he's one of a kind, out of step with his peers and probably suffering for it more than you know. At the Music School he'd be *encouraged* to develop his individuality, to interact with kids who are on much the same wavelength. But of course that would mean someone other than you influencing the boy, and you can't have that, can you? He must want what *you* want.'

David's anger, once released, built from strength to strength until he was raging up and down the room like a bear, his disgust evident with every word. Hands on hips, Clare smouldered under the unjustified attack, marshalling her own angry ammunition. David came to a halt in front of her, staring down his arrogant nose, his black eyes savage with frustration.

'Oh, yes, you're just aching to order me out again, aren't you? To pretend that nothing happened. Well, *I* happened, Clare Malcolm. And I dare you to try and deny my words, *or* the fact that ten minutes ago over there on the floor, you gave me the right to say them!'

Clare faced him proudly. 'I gave you the right to nothing but the use of my body!' She ignored his dangerous, hissing breath. 'And as it happened I *have* sought the proper advice for Tim. He had several months of therapy with a child psychologist, whose final diagnosis was that Tim would naturally grow out of his fears, given a stable living environment. And over the past six months he *has* improved dramatically. It's only when he's under par that he has a tendency to revert.'

'Then why in the hell didn't you tell me that when I asked?' David roared, outraged at being cheated of the satisfaction of being right.

'Maybe if you had asked the question without implying you already knew the answer, I might have,' Clare retorted.

'Hell, you can be an aggravating bitch!'

'If you're going to insult me, have the courtesy to do it in a language I don't understand. Tamara isn't the only vicious-tongued Deverenko.'

David wasn't about to let her consolidate her victory. 'But I was right about the rest, wasn't I? I can talk until I'm blue in the face, and you won't budge an inch. I wouldn't put it past you to keep Tim buried down here just to spite me,' he said sullenly.

'You're not so important in my life that I would bother,' said Clare loftily, but she couldn't resist dipping a flaming torch to the bridge she had just mentally doused with accelerant. 'Although as it happens I've decided that the school *might* be best for Tim, after all.'

'What?'

Clare was unnerved by the brightness of the conflagration she had caused, and hurriedly backed off. 'I said *might*. I'd have to know a lot more about it first...before I made my final decision...'

CHAPTER EIGHT

CLARE sipped her glass of wine and smiled warmly at the handsome but tiresomely intense young man who had been talking her ear off for the past half-hour. It was tough appearing fascinated when she was in danger of dropping off to sleep, but it was a matter of pride as well as gratitude that she conceal her boredom. The young man had rescued her from the intimidating curiosity of all those who had seen her arrive at the elegant soirée on David Deverenko's arm. The guest list was a who's who of music in Auckland, and so far the boring young man, an accountant, was the only other person Clare had met who shared her tenuous connection with the main topic of conversation of the evening—his girlfriend of two weeks was a cello player with the NZSO. The rescue, Clare sensed, was mutual...two philistines adrift in a sea of culture.

To give the devil his due, David had stayed by her side for the first hour, introducing her to all and sundry, but Clare was at her worst in large crowds of strangers. Although she knew she was looking her best in the hurriedly bought black dress, she feared that she had come across as the archetypal dumb blonde with hardly a word to say as the informed discussions about music and musicians ebbed and flowed around her. It would have eased her tongue-tied shyness if she had known that, far from thinking her dumb, the grapevine had already labelled her an intriguing mystery, cool and serene and so confident of her hold on the guest of honour that she could afford to be laid back.

Clare nodded vaguely at something the young man said, her eyes discreetly seeking out David's dark head. She found him in his natural element, surrounded by a

138

trio of adoring women. As if she had touched him he looked up and, across the heads of the chattering groups of people between them, Clare felt the impact of his accusing stare. She felt a renewed stirring of resentment. What did he have to be annoyed about? *She* was the one who had had this sprung on her at the last moment. *She* was the one who had had to put up with his impossible moodiness during their brief trip to Auckland. Defiantly she raised her glass to him in a cool toast, and smiled even more warmly at the young man, so that he momentarily lost the thread of his long-winded story.

Clare had expected David to be all charm on this visit. After all, he was supposed to be persuading her in favour of his school, not infuriating her to the point that she wished never to see him again. Well, *almost* to the point.

He had certainly been quick enough to capitalise on her surprising change of mind about the Music School. No one could accuse David of procrastinating. Hardly were the words out of Clare's mouth before he had organised this weekend. It was impossible just to *describe* his school, it seemed; one had to see it in action. And this weekend was the perfect time. Usually most of the children went home at weekends, at least the ones whose homes were within reasonable distance, but a series of special weekend concerts by the pupils had been organised to coincide with the Auckland Arts festival. Clare's own feeble attempts at procrastination—how could she leave Tim when the doctor had pronounced a bad cold? How could David leave Tamara when she was still wrapped in furious, silent hostility towards both of them?—were summarily dismissed. Miles was back. He would do her job for her and keep an eye on Tim and Tamara, and lend them the Dauphin and a pilot into the bargain. Clare had been literally swept off her feet, and in no time at all was waving out the window of the helicopter's luxurious passenger cabin at a very stiff-upper-lipped Tim as he stood in the curve of Miles's arm. He hadn't said much when she'd told him about the purpose of her trip, but she could see that he was both excited and disturbed by the possibilities. He was too intelligent not to realise that there was a price attached to the dream. David's autobiography had dealt in detail on the Music School, and Tim knew that residence was one of the rules. How would he react if possibility became reality? Clare didn't know, and neither did Tim, and she sensed that was something that bothered him. Tim was usually quick to make up his mind. Indecisiveness was not something he subscribed to, particularly when it involved anything to do with his musical obsession.

Clare had to swallow a lump in her throat as she watched the figures recede in a swirl of cross-winds from the rotor blades.

'He'll be all right. Miles will keep him busy. And he knows where to get in touch with you,' David had told her abruptly, reading her thoughts. He had been strangely curt all through breakfast. Perhaps he was worried about his daughter, who had predictably been absent from the farewell.

'Did you talk to Tamara?'

He shook his head broodingly. The girl had been avoiding everyone since the confrontation in Clare's suite two nights before. 'I talked *at* her. I don't know if she took any of it in. She didn't even ask if she could come.'

'Perhaps you should have brought her, anyway.'

'And have her sabotage the whole weekend? Clare, I could reason with her until Kingdom-come—she'll hear only what she wants to, those things that reinforce her prejudices about you, about me, about the world of conspiracy that stops her being happy. We'll be back tomorrow evening, and perhaps by then she might have calmed down enough to open the lines of communication. I want her to realise that it's herself she's punishing, more than me, with this silent treatment.'

'You...you did tell her that nothing happened...' Clare began, trailing off unhappily when he measured her with a look.

'But something did happen, Clare.'

'Well, I hope you told her that we wouldn't be... I mean that I'll be staying at Virginia's while you're at the school.'

'But you're not.'

'W... what?'

That had been the first shock. That David had rung Virginia and told her of a change of plan. To fully appreciate the family atmosphere of the school, Clare would be spending the night there.

'But...I...'

'It's all arranged, so you may as well save your breath,' David told her with a hard-edged satisfaction that struck an oddly discordant note. 'Virginia's on my side on this one; she'd make your life hell if you tried to stay there now. She wants the school to grab every chance it can get to convince you of its merits.'

'I could book in at a hotel,' Clare said loftily, knowing that he was right.

'Then make sure it's a double room, because where you go, I go.'

His presumption was galling. 'If you think I'm going to Auckland for any reason other than to look at the school——'

'You mean like a little sexual fling? I wouldn't dream of it. The chaste Widow Malcolm? Unthinkable! Don't worry, Clare, your priceless virtue will be safe at the school. No late-night visitors allowed in the staff bedrooms. We have to set a good example for the children; you know how embarrassingly honest *they* can be. You'll be quite safe. Lonely, maybe, but safe...'

Clare was bewildered by his sarcasm. All right, so she had jumped to the conclusion he wanted her to stay at his house and was offended by it; there was no need for him to sneer at her prudery. Clare turned away from him to look out the window at the rolling green countryside gliding below. She shouldn't feel betrayed. She had known all along what he wanted. Still, to hear it put in such crude terms, as a 'fling', was like a knife in her wary heart. She wished she could order the pilot to turn

around and take her back, but she couldn't act so self-
ishly. For Tim's sake she had to go through with this,
and do her best to judge the school with an unbiased
eye.

The rest of the short, interminable flight was passed
in silence. Several times Clare felt David looking at her,
but she refused to meet his gaze. He could damned well
apologise if he expected her to be civil. Just because she
loved him didn't mean that he could walk all over her!

The helicopter had special permission to land in the
huge, park-like grounds of the school, and Clare was for
once relieved at the sight of a bunch of strangers waiting
to welcome them. David was the essence of politeness
as he introduced her to several of the teaching and
household staff, relaxing into a warmth of smiles as he
answered the shouted questions of the excited children
as they inspected the impressive helicopter. David introduced them, too, all by name without having to fumble
for an identity even once, and Clare was amused at the
enthusiastic offers to show her around. David brushed
them off with a casual authority, and then selected three
of the older children who could be spared from the festival rehearsal. One of them, a teenage boy, had a gravity
that reminded her of Tim, but the other two, a girl and
a boy, were completely unawed by the task of escorting
their beloved maestro and his guest. They were vocal
guides, and Clare was soon overwhelmed by their eager
friendliness, and their pride in 'their' school. She was
shown a lavish array of equipment, and informed that
there were only six to eight children in each class. Several
timetables ran simultaneously throughout the day to cater
to the different age levels, so that both music-rooms and
school-rooms were constantly in use by one class or
another. Studying them, Clare had to agree that they
were marvellously efficient. Timetables were considered
by staff and pupils alike as both sacrosanct and an in-
joke. Clare hadn't really believed David's grandiose
claims that the school was like an enlarged family, but
after joining the children for lunch in the big dining-

room—a simple, wholesome meal of vegetable soup, salad, brown bread, fruit and cheese—and wandering around the rest of the school and grounds she had to admit that she hadn't found a single thing to criticise. The children seemed immensely at ease with themselves and each other, and full of a loyal camaraderie that didn't even resent forfeiting a free weekend at home in favour of representing the school at the festival.

When David excused himself to attend to some business with the musical director, Clare had a short meeting with the principal and was then shown to a small, attractive room near the kitchen by Brenda Sutcliffe, the matron.

She was very chatty and informative, and apologised for the smallness of the room. 'But we have quite a few parents here this weekend, so we just have to make do.'

'If it's a problem, I could go and stay with my mother-in-law——' Clare began.

'Oh, no, it's no problem,' Brenda said warmly. A short, motherly-looking woman in her mid-fifties, she was obviously used to soothing both parents and children. 'At a pinch we can always avail ourselves of the extra rooms at David's, but I try and avoid that if I can. The poor man gets little enough privacy as it is. He really is marvellously tolerant...with children, anyway.' A small, conspiratorial smile. 'It's the adults he tends to get testy with.'

'I know the feeling,' said Clare drily.

'Oh, he'll be on his best behaviour with you,' Brenda reassured her innocently. 'He always is when he has his eye on someone special.'

Clare nearly blushed, then she realised that Brenda was talking about Tim. Of course David wouldn't have been so blatant as to say he had his eye on the mother for reasons other than his precious school!

'Well, I'll leave you to unpack. The bathroom is just down the hall to your left. Because of the concert we're just having a snack at five-thirty, our usual dinner-time in winter, and the proper meal when they come back;

but I'll make sure you and David have something more substantial. From my very meagre experience, these society parties don't usually feed you more than prissy bites until the wee hours.'

'Society party?' Clare looked at Brenda blankly.

'Oh, dear, is it supposed to be a surprise? David didn't tell me not to mention it.' Brenda sighed. 'For a man who lives such a highly organised life, he can be annoyingly forgetful sometimes. He said that you and he would be going on from the concert to a private party at the Regent. Some sort of posh fund-raiser for the youth arm of the NZSO.'

If David had forgotten to mention it, Clare was sure the omission was deliberate, another attempt at manipulation.

'Well, he didn't say anything to me, so naturally I didn't bring anything suitable to wear. I couldn't possibly go.'

'Oh, but you have to! Everyone's expecting David to be there——'

'David, yes, but not me,' said Clare firmly.

Or she *thought* she had been firm. An hour later she was in the boutique of a friend of one of the visiting parents, trying on a selection of very exclusive and expensive dresses—offered at a generous 'family' discount—the shock of David's reaction to her refusal ringing in her ears.

When she had finally run the elusive Russian to earth in a conference with his principal and his music director, he had told her calmly that it was fine; if she didn't go, he wouldn't either.

The two men with him had looked at Clare with renewed interest, as she floundered in her embarrassment.

'David, don't be ridiculous. You can't not go just because I don't have a dress. Take someone else.'

'I don't want to take anyone else. And if a dress is your only problem, that's easily solved.'

Clare's mouth tightened into a little knot of annoyance, and David's eyelids drooped. 'Or perhaps you're trying to let me down lightly. Perhaps you have another date for the night?'

She would have liked to have claimed one, but those narrowed dark eyes warned her not to lie. She sensed that David would have no qualms about dragging the details from her in front of his interested staff.

'I...I'm just not very good at parties,' she said truthfully.

'I can take or leave them myself. Which shall we do to this one?' And as she hesitated he added silkily, 'You must know by now, Clare—I can be *twice* as stubborn as ever you can...'

Hence the black dress, defiantly demure with its high-necked, cross-over bodice and long, slim skirt. Demure, that was, until she moved and the dramatic slit up one side revealed a breathtaking amount of thigh. Even the self-absorbed accountant couldn't help his gaze wandering down every time Clare shifted her weight, and she did so now, just to break the monotony. After six years of faithful wedded bliss and two of celibacy, in the space of a single evening she had apparently become a mindless sex object!

An arm slid around her waist, and then the accountant's eyes jerked guiltily up as Clare was drawn briefly back against a hard body.

'Sorry to break this up, but I have some people I want you to meet, darling,' David's voice shafted past her ear, sounding anything but apologetic. The young man actually took a step back at the stony, black-Russian stare. 'Excuse us, won't you?' It was a command, not a request, and Clare found herself marched unceremoniously away.

'How dare you——?' she stuttered.

'Ten seconds later and you would have been swimming in drool. Couldn't you find someone more mature to cosy up in corners with?'

Clare gaped at his rigid profile, but before she could voice her outrage she was forced to smile stiffly at a new set of introductions. So furious was she with the cavalier way that David was behaving that she had trouble keeping up with the polite conversation that followed. When she was asked whether she knew many people in Auckland, after explaining that she was visiting from Rotorua, she murmured that she had lost touch with most of her old friends, but that most of her late husband's family were Aucklanders.

'What about Julian? You've kept in touch with him, haven't you?' David interjected, irritated by her cold-shouldered vagueness in front of his friends. 'Or perhaps he's family, though I'm sure the "uncle" is only an honorary title.'

'Uncle Julian?' At least he had her attention now. Clare was staring at him in horror. Surely he wasn't going to embarrass her in such sophisticated company.

David's smile was not reassuring. 'Tim told me *all* about him. I'm surprised you didn't bring him along tonight. I'm sure he must be fascinating company...'

Clare would never have believed that David could be so small-minded. She was blushing brilliantly at the speculation she sensed around her, cringing inside at what they would all think if David kept up his taunting. If they had thought she was a dumb blonde before, they would consider her a real case of arrested mental development if he told them... Suddenly her hideous embarrassment was swamped by anger. This really was the last straw!

'Well, I must admit, after an evening in *your* company, I realise I infinitely prefer his. At least he's always there when I need him, which happens to be right now. If you'll all excuse me?' she said with a glacial dignity that awed those of the group with personal experience of the Russian temperament now openly smouldering. 'I have a pressing engagement elsewhere.'

Aware that she was making something of a spectacle of herself, but too angry to care, Clare sailed across the room, closely followed by a furious Deverenko.

He caught her in the cavernous foyer of the hotel, where staff, who were trained to discreetly ignore public displays of the personal problems of the rich and famous, pretended not to notice.

'Where are you going?'

'Back to the school.' There were no taxis at the front, and the uniformed doorman was so busy being discreet that she had to tap him on the shoulder to request him to do his job.

'If you can *bear* to wait a few minutes for me to get my coat, I'll come with you,' said David tautly.

Sure the pun was an intentional sneer, Clare rounded on him. 'No, thanks, I've had enough of your company for one night. I don't know what the matter is with you, but I don't have to put up with your attacks of temperament! I came up to Auckland, I came here tonight, because *you* insisted. You're the one who walked off and left me in a crowd of strangers. What did you expect me to do, twiddle my thumbs and wait for you to notice me again? In Rotorua you couldn't wait to get me on that helicopter, and yet ever since we took off you've treated me as if I've committed some *sin*——'

'And we all know how impossible that is——'

'There you go again. If you have something on your mind, say it! Don't hide behind snide remarks and hints.' Clare's voice echoed against the glass wall facing the street, and she consciously tried to lower it.

David had no such reservations. He turned to face her, eyes smoking as he demanded, 'Why didn't you want to come with me tonight?'

'I told you,' said Clare tightly. 'I don't enjoy big parties.'

'Perhaps if you made an effort you might surprise yourself. After all, you manage to socialise quite easily with all the strangers who flit through Moonlight. But you didn't want to enjoy yourself tonight, did you? You were just aching for an excuse to walk out.'

'I don't know what you're talking about,' hissed Clare furiously, although in a way he was right. She hadn't made any special effort to join in. Instead she had allowed herself to be overwhelmed by her own sense of inadequacy.

'Oh, no? I bet you made a phone call this evening, before the concert.'

'Well, yes, I——' She had called Virginia, and promised to drop in and see her before they went back to Rotorua.

'And was Julian pleased to hear from you?'

'*Julian?*'

'Why the secrecy? Could it be that the sweet, ever-faithful madonna is feeling a little guilty about her *affair*? I can accept that your sex drive didn't die with your husband, Clare, but wasn't it rather tacky to fall into bed with someone else even before he was gone? Tim said you and Uncle Julian were sleeping together while his father was in hospital...'

Clare felt the blood drain from her face. For a moment she thought she was going to faint. 'W...what exactly did Tim tell you?' she croaked, white-lipped.

David was equally pale, under the olive complexion, the fury seeming to have drained out of him now he had tapped the raging conflictions that had been festering inside him during the last twelve hours: jealousy, dis-illusionment, frustration, contempt and sheer male pique...none of them had quite banished the hope and fierce desire. Dammit! If he'd known he had a flesh and blood rival, he might have handled everything differently...

'Ironic, really,' he said. 'We had a pre-breakfast chat this morning in which I was trying, in a roundabout way, to reassure him about your going away. We discussed loneliness and the different ways that people coped with it. We agreed that music was a good focus for negative as well as positive feelings. And we went deeper into the subject of personal loss, and Tim said that when his father got sick and went into hospital that you used to cry at nights until you started sleeping with Uncle Julian. You often sleep with Uncle Julian when you get lonely, he said. You tell him your troubles and he keeps you

warm the way that Lee used to. No wonder Tim is so
frank about sex! But why make it a big secret? Don't
you realise that you must be confusing the hell out of
him? After telling me that, he clammed up and made
me promise not to tell anyone. Why is it so important
that nobody knows? After all, your husband has been
gone two years now. What's stopping you getting
together openly? Is it because the illicit freedom of an
affair gives you a kick? Or is Julian married? Is that it,
Clare? Are you having an affair with a married man?'

'No. But I almost had one with an idiot! You sancti-
monious——' Words failed her. She ought to have put
him straight right there and then, but the thought of all
that he had put her through that day because of a simple
misunderstanding that could have been cleared up with
a few words enraged her. That he could think she was
so...so underhanded and lacking in morals——

She simmered all the way back to the school, alone
in the back seat of the cab, savouring the expression of
blank outrage David had been wearing when she had
slipped past him and slammed the car door in his face,
after sweetly informing him that she was going to spend
the night with Julian.

And to think of all the tossing and turning she had
done the last few nights, worrying about whether she
should forget her doubts and scruples this weekend and
succumb to the temptation that would inevitably arise!
And, from the dog-in-the-manger way he had acted, he
had obviously hoped for the same, even though he
thought she was in the middle of a secret adulterous affair
with another man. In his sophisticated world, such a
ménage à trois might be commonplace, but not in *hers*.

The black dress was replaced by a bewitching yellow
silk teddy and matching robe—which she blushed to
admit she had packed in anticipation of David's admiration—and Clare ruthlessly scrubbed off her make-up
in the bathroom along the hall before slamming back to
her lonely room. The trouble was, she didn't feel in the
least like sleep. She wanted to have a good rage or a

good cry, and couldn't decide which would be more beneficial. She wished she was back at Moonlight, in familiar surroundings. She ached for the lost innocence of loving only Lee. After a great deal of pacing and muttering, she sighed and smiled wryly at the comforting hump in the bed.

'At least I've still got you, Uncle Julian. Looks like it's just going to be the two of us.'

At first the knock on the door was so tentative that she hardly heard it. She hesitated, and decided it couldn't be David. David, particularly in the mood in which she had left him, would never be tentative. She knew that some of the staff and parents were still up and about because she had heard chatter and the clink of crockery in the kitchen.

It *was* David.

'What do you want?'

He smiled as tentatively as he had knocked, and Clare had a very clear image of hastily donned sheep's clothing. 'I had no right to say those things. I lost my temper. I'm glad you decided to come back here.'

The hint of satisfaction in the soft words stiffened Clare's spine. 'It's late and I'm tired. You can do your grovelling in the morning.' She tried to close the door, but it wasn't a sheep's hoof that slammed against it. Clare looked from the strong, flat hand to the dark Slavonic face.

'Clare, please. My mother always used to warn me against letting the sun go down on an argument.'

'It's nearly midnight, the sun went down hours ago,' Clare pointed out tartly.

'If you let me in, I'll explain——'

Clare thought of the lump in the bed behind her, and tightened her hand nervously on the doorhandle. 'In the morning.' Unfortunately her voice wavered and she could feel a blush sneaking up her throat. David's eyes sharpened. He tried to look beyond her into the room, and she made the mistake of trying to narrow the gap in the door to prevent him. The sheepskin slid to the floor and the wolf, or rather the bear, showed its savage teeth.

'What are you trying to hide, Clare?'

'Nothing.' Her flush mounted at the lie. David's eyes sank to the loving yellow silk.

'The hell you aren't! Did you bring your lover here, to flaunt in my face? Let me in.' It was the merest of courtesies, because they both knew she couldn't stop him.

He stood in the middle of the small room, taking in the comfortable furnishings in a predatory sweep. 'Where is he, Clare?'

'You have no right——'

'I told you the rules. No visitors.'

'You're visiting,' she pointed out, edging towards the bed as he moved, carefully keeping between David and the lump under the covers.

He looked at her, flushed and nervous, backing away from him, not realising that the lamp behind her was revealing the sheerness of the French silk. His smile was a slow threat. 'I *make* the rules, so I get to police them. In the closet?' He matched the sudden demand with an equally sudden movement, and flung open the door of the built-in wardrobe. If Clare hadn't been so angry and offended, she would have laughed.

'You're making a complete fool of yourself, David.' She perched on the edge of the bed and felt behind her to pull up the sheet she had turned down earlier, but she had forgotten the mirror on the wall by the closet. David turned and in two strides was towering over her, reaching past her to rip the sheet back down.

He stared at the bright, enquiring brown eyes, as dark as his own, looking up at him from the pillow. For a full thirty seconds he stared in silence. Then he looked at Clare, whose pretended nonchalance was ruined by her hectic colour and quivering mouth.

He sat down beside her on the bed and placed the teddy bear on to his knees. The bear was wearing striped pyjamas with a very enlightening monogram embroidered on the jacket.

'J.' David traced the thread. 'Now what could that stand for I wonder? John? Jake? Joseph?'

Clare averted her face. David's voice was very soft, very controlled. Dangerously so. She sensed that to laugh or to taunt him now with his folly would push him over the edge. And he was waiting, wanting to be pushed...

'Or... could it be... Julian?' The softness congealed into a thin sheet of ice. 'Aren't you going to introduce me to your... friend, Clare?'

Clare risked a tiny step on to the slick surface. 'It's not really mine. It's Tim's. But he... he gave it to me.'

'To keep you company?'

'S-something like that.' All her desire to laugh was gone. David was stroking the bear's soft hand, and the way his fingers slid through the silky fur was unnervingly evocative.

'So this is Uncle Julian whom you sleep with?'

'Y-yes.' She didn't trust that mildness, not in conjunction with the fierce tension in the big body. 'You...you were the one who jumped to conclusions...'

'Forgivable in the circumstances, wouldn't you say?' David seemed absorbed in his stroking of the bear. Clare felt a ridiculously possessive surge of resentment. She wanted to snatch the bear out of those magic hands lest Uncle Julian, too, find himself seduced.

'You could have *asked*...'

David turned his head and she forgot to breathe. Oh, there was anger there, and resentment, but a smouldering excitement, too.

'I did ask,' he pointed out.

'You deliberately embarrassed me in front of everyone. You...you made me angry.'

'That's nothing to what you made me. You told me there was no one besides Lee, and suddenly your son is chattering on about some mysterious man with whom you seemed to be deeply and secretly involved. I was jealous. I was afraid I'd explode if it turned out to be the truth.'

'You did,' pointed out Clare recklessly.

'Oh, that wasn't an explosion, Clare. That was just a minor eruption. The explosion is yet to come. Did you wear that beautiful piece of silk for me?'

'No,' she said weakly. 'All my nightwear is...is...'

'Sexy? It's wasted on Uncle Julian. He strikes me as very much of a bear's bear.' David arranged the furry limbs to his liking. 'You need someone who can not only listen but respond. A woman like you could never be fulfilled by a platonic relationship that's all give and no take. Uncle Julian is all very well for a cuddle or two, but he has a fatal flaw.'

'Oh?' The word stuck in her throat.

David sat the bear on the bedside-table.

'He's not Russian.'

'Oh...' It came out in a sighing rush as she met the promise of his eyes.

'Russian bears have bad tempers, but they make up for it in other ways.'

'W...what ways?'

The sullen, sensuous beauty of his features blurred as he bent towards her to demonstrate. His mouth wasn't gentle, but she didn't want it to be. There was too much dammed-up passion intermingled with the vestiges of their anger to waste time in the tender preliminaries. For a long time they kissed, falling back to entwine on the bed, David shrugging out of his dinner-jacket and white shirt, removing Clare's robe so that he could murmur foreign phrases of delight at the loveliness beneath.

'Speak English,' Clare whispered, holding out her arms to welcome him back.

David held back, sitting beside her outstretched body, enjoying the agony of anticipation which had racked him for days and which was now whipped to its peak. 'If you understood what I was saying, what I want to do to you and how, you'd blush for a week.'

Clare's eyes were a smoky grey. 'Tell me...show me...' she invited huskily, more uninhibited than she had ever been in her life. Her body throbbed languorously under his hungry, desiring gaze. 'Please, I don't want to wait any more...'

The thick muscles of his chest and flat belly clenched. David leant over and turned the love-worn brown teddy bear's face to the wall.

'There are some things ordinary bears shouldn't know. It might make them discontented with their lot.' The low, sensuous words shivered over Clare's skin, and she gave a tiny cry as she felt the warm hand slide caressingly up her thighs.

'Beautiful legs...' He made her lie there while he admired them, worshipped them with hands and eyes and mouth, from the sensitive inner curve of her ankle to the palest, silky-soft skin at the top of her thighs where the loose ruffle of yellow lace could be coaxed to reveal its secrets.

He seemed to sense the moment when she couldn't bear any more, and reluctantly returned to her mouth, her breasts gleaming against the parted silk of the thin bodice, cupped in the darkness of his exquisitely knowledgeable hands. Clare felt the heaviness of him, knew the taste of his desire, and wanted him more than she had wanted anything in her life, with an urgency that was as exhilarating as it was frightening. He seemed to know her body better than she did herself, and she ached to gain that intimate knowledge of him. She revelled in the freedom to tease him as she eluded his caresses so that she could take off the rest of his clothes. After she had knelt on the bed to remove his shoes and socks, she laughingly restrained him from kissing and stroking her aching breasts while she attacked his trousers.

'You must let me take *some* of the initiative, David,' she told him, deliciously arousing in her innocent haste, 'otherwise I shall feel like a puppet, with you pulling the strings.'

'I rather had in mind a glove puppet,' said David wickedly, taking advantage of her vulnerable position to run his hand up the rounded curve of her buttock under the leg of her now considerably dishevelled teddy.

'I mean it, David,' said Clare, slapping his hand away, half-serious in her attempt to have him realise that she wanted to *share* the act of love, not just be a passive participant. Her tongue curled out of the corner of her mouth and she concentrated on fathoming the mystery of his fashionable cummerbund. Suddenly, with her smooth, silky skin and freckles and slightly awed eagerness, she seemed very young. Just so did Tim use his tongue to help concentrate when he was struggling with a new practice piece. David stilled beneath her slender hands. He had set out to seduce her and he had succeeded beyond his wildest dreams. She was like a pale, searing flame in his arms. He had wanted her like this...had imagined how it would be. But imagination was different from reality. In reality one had responsibilities, to oneself and to others.

'Clare.' It caused a physical pain to draw her hands away from his hardness. He kissed the tender tips, holding her when she would have pulled away still smiling, teasing...

'Clare, we can't do this,' he sighed.

She thought he was joking, teasing her, heightening the pleasure in what was to come. He closed his eyes to shut out her sinfully sweet pout. He must be mad to do this...to give her the rope to hang him. He had never considered himself the self-sacrificing type before!

'Clare, have you made up your mind about Tim and the school?' He opened his eyes. He *was* mad! 'Clare, don't look at me like that. I want you, heaven knows there's not much chance of me hiding that. But I don't want you to claim afterwards that I was trying to influence you unfairly——'

Clare's heart began to beat again, the stinging humiliation fading as quickly as it had come. 'I wouldn't think that! I'm quite capable of separating sex from...from the rest of our lives.'

It was not a very diplomatic lie, face-saving though it might have been. David put her quite firmly from him and began to dress. 'But I'm not. It isn't going to be that easy, for either of us. I demand more than just neatly compartmentalised sex, so you'd better be very sure before you blithely throw yourself into my arms. And I want this other business with Tim sorted out so that we can concentrate purely on *us*.'

Clare was in no mood for his exquisite reason. Now she was aching with unrequited desire as well as love! 'It must be very convenient to be able to switch on and off the way you obviously do——'

He scooped her up against his broad chest, and before she had time to get excited again pulled back the bed-clothes and dumped her on the sheet, tucking her in with ruthless efficiency. 'Clare, darling, right now I'm very tempted to lock those gorgeous legs around me and throw away the key. Here!' He thrust Uncle Julian in beside her, and gave the teddy bear a sullen, jealous glare that eased the hard lump in Clare's hollow breast. He actually resented a stuffed toy—the Martyred Maestro!

'Enjoy her while you can, furball; your days are seriously numbered!' he growled. The look he turned on Clare melted her to the pillow. 'Decide soon, Clare. My heart isn't strong enough to stand this kind of strain.'

Neither is mine, thought Clare sadly as she tried to will herself to sleep. She had already decided about Tim . . . it was her own plans that were up in the air. She couldn't stay at Moonlight while Tim lived in Auckland, and she didn't want to move in with Virginia, who would probably expect it. Still, she had heard one or two things today that might help. Tomorrow. . .tomorrow she would tell David that Tim would be joining his select band of pupils. Tomorrow morning. That would give she and David the rest of the day to concentrate on '*us*'.

Like many a best-laid plan, it was not to be. For Clare was woken the next morning by a pale-faced, distracted David. Tamara had walked into the bush last night from the lodge and not walked out again. Miles had called out Search and Rescue, and the helicopter was fuelled-up and ready to go. . .

CHAPTER NINE

IT WASN'T raining any more, but the air was still thick with moisture and the ground near the jetty had been churned into a muddy mess by a clutch of four-wheel-drive vehicles and the heavy, tramping boots of the searchers.

An air of uneasy relief hung over the site as the team of Search and Rescue workers began to withdraw. They had gone out at first light, but hadn't found Tamara until late afternoon. She had been warmly dressed, but she hadn't banked on the rain which had accompanied the plunge in night temperature, or the rustling of nocturnal animals that had had her stumbling around in the impenetrable dark instead of being comfortably curled up in her carefully planned 'hidey-hole', waiting to be rescued.

For Tamara had deliberately 'lost' herself, and in doing so had underestimated the bush. She had thought that she could walk out as easily as she had walked in, once she had sufficiently frightened everyone. She was showing the first signs of exposure by the time she was found, and in her distraught state had sobbed out the truth, earning herself an angry lecture from the police officer in charge of the search. Tamara had taken it on the chin, stiff and proud, although she had apologised in a choked voice that was sincere in its shame and fright.

Clare had expected her to throw herself at her father then, since after all the object of the exercise had been to get his full attention, but Tamara had taken one look at his weary face, full of shock, sadness and disappointment, and launched herself instead at a startled Clare. When her father had touched her she had actually flinched, and Clare had instinctively cradled her

protectively closer. David went white under his olive skin
and his eyes revealed a chilling pain that was swiftly
superseded by a resentful resignation that Clare had no
difficulty in interpreting. Ironically, with this last gesture
of futility, Tamara had achieved her aim. She had rendered her father powerless. He was jealous. Whatever
the difficulties between them, he was her *father*, and it
should have been to David that she turned in time of
greatest woe.

It took Clare an hour to calm Tamara down, while
David reluctantly made himself scarce. Tamara couldn't
stop talking. It all poured out, how ashamed David was
of her, how he must despise and hate her for screwing
up his life. Her wild, thoughtless scheme to bring him
rushing to her side had backfired horribly. She de-
stroyed everything she touched. Her father would never
love her the way he used to. He couldn't. She had humiliated him once too often, failed him too many times.

'Funny, that's just what he said—that he had failed
you,' Clare told the sobbing girl as she guided her into
a hot bath. 'He's not perfect, you know, just because
he's an adult. He feels the same kind of hurt and con-
fusion that you do. And you're both wrong, anyway.
You can't talk about love in terms of success or failure.
It's not an examination subject. You just do the best
you can as you go along. And you certainly don't try to
use it to control those you love. The only person you
can *really* control is yourself, and you did pretty well
out there, Tamara. You'd done something stupid but
you faced up to it; you didn't try to run away. People
respect that. Maybe you've learnt that running away only
presents you with a new set of problems to face. And
maybe you'll soon realise that your father isn't some
superhuman being who can solve all those problems for
you. He's as much a victim of circumstance as you are.
Think about it.'

She left Tamara to soak and brood, meeting David
coming into the newly redecorated suite that they had
moved into a few days before Miles's return.

'She's in the bath,' said Clare huskily. 'I've ordered her some soup and a hot drink——'

'So have I. I *am* capable of looking after her physical needs, at least,' he said curtly. He hadn't even stopped to shave that morning, and the dark growth added aggression to his tense features. Clare forgave him his touchiness, for she had been with him during those long, grey hours of nail-biting anxiety and heard him lash himself with guilt: for leaving Tamara when he knew she was upset, for his impatience in brushing aside her needs, for not making enough concessions to her youth and vulnerability. Clare hadn't dared to offer any easy platitudes, silently accepting his raging self-contempt as a way to keep his worst fears at bay. Like a wounded bear in a trap, he would blindly lash out at any attempt to help. Now anger at the needlessness of his suffering was probably compounding his guilt. He needed to vent it before he faced his daughter.

'Of course you are,' said Clare carefully. She wanted to ease the burden, to tell him it was instinctive to seek sympathy from one's own sex. 'But——'

'But you don't trust me any more than Tamara does to understand. I can imagine what's going through your mind. That I had it coming to me. So much for my theories on juvenile independence. I bet you're congratulating yourself that you didn't let me seduce you into parting you and Tim. Tamara almost died because she felt that I had abandoned her,' he said jerkily.

'David, about Tim...' Amid the tense excitement of the day, she had found time to take Tim aside and gently break the news. Although he was still dubious about living with strangers, his mind had been eased when Clare explained that, naturally, she would be moving to Auckland, too, if the school accepted Tim. She didn't want to hint *how* close until she had investigated the possibility further. The *if* had been a clincher. Tim's stubbornness reared its head. It became a matter of Malcolm pride that he not suffer the mortification of rejection.

'Forget it, Clare. Forget everything I ever said. Now, if you'll excuse me, my daughter and I need some time alone together. I want her to relate to *me*, not hide behind a stranger's sympathy. And you can tell your boss that we'll be leaving tomorrow.'

Forget *everything*? Clare was still choking on that the next morning as she jogged towards the lodge along the lake edge. Did he mean Tim, or literally *everything*? And to call her a stranger, in that casual, dismissive voice. That was a lethal blow. Twice she had offered him her body and twice he had made excuses not to take it— good excuses at the time, but maybe they were just a way to avoid the embarrassment of turning her down flat!

'Clare?' She shied. David was hovering on the steps to the lodge. His wary expression changed to shock as he saw the damp patches on her track-suit, her wet hair, and the towel in her hand. 'Did you fall in the lake?'

As if he cared if she drowned! 'I've been swimming.'

'In the *lake*? In the middle of winter? You must be crazy!'

'No, just fit. Are you all packed?' she forced herself to ask.

'All the commercial flights are full, so we're staying another day.' So he had meant it, every word! Clare fought to appear calm. 'Aren't you scared of hypothermia and cramp?' David continued.

'I don't go out of my depth and I don't stay in for long. But I wouldn't recommend it for someone like you.' Her anger at her stupidity for falling in love with him came out like scorn.

'Why not? I'm a very good swimmer.' His response to the challenge was reflexive, and it encouraged her to goad further.

'Sure. In a nice, antiseptic pool heated to blood temperature. Out in the open you have to be a bit tough. You're out of your element here, David.' In more ways than one.

She swept past him, ignoring his 'We'll see about that!' and an hour later was savouring the sweet taste of revenge when she was drawn out of her office by a commotion in the foyer.

'You must be crazy, man!' Miles was booming at a rigid and distinctly blue-tinted David. 'That lake's pretty cold in summer, let alone in winter! Nobody's *that* masochistic!'

David unlocked his teeth as he saw Clare, and stuttered with icy triumph, 'Clare is...she told me...next bay.'

'Clare?' Miles did a double-take at her guilty blush.

David saw it, too. 'S...she was there, this morning.' He shuddered. His jeans and sweater offered no warmth to his bloodless skin.

'But not in the lake, old man! Didn't she tell you about the pool?' Miles's voice shivered at the joke. 'At the far end, in that rocky section of bank, there's a thermal spring that feeds into the lake. There's a hot pool and a warm patch of lake shallows. Hey, Davey, you've got some guts!' Miles slapped him gleefully on the back. 'Come into the bar and sit by the fire. I'll get you a couple of dozen whiskies to warm up. Did I tell you that I once spent a few weeks down in Antarctica? They said it was summer, but...' His voice faded as he towed a tottering David towards the reviving heat. The murderous expression frozen on to the violinist's blue-lipped face made Clare giggle nervously. He heard, his stiff-legged gait faltering momentarily, and Clare suddenly felt a heady excitement at the knowledge that this time she had made a fool of *him*.

Her excitement fizzled when he made no attempt to confront her. David in a rage was at least preferable to no David at all. But for the rest of the day he stayed in his room. Making international phone calls and arguing about something with Efrem, a very subdued Tamara said, when she insisted on accompanying Clare to her 'jazzercise' class, after convincing her that she was suffering no ill-effects from her self-inflicted adventure.

Tamara didn't say anything else about her father, and Clare tactfully avoiding any probing, but when David didn't join them for dinner she couldn't resist asking whether they had talked.

Tamara nodded, tearing herself away from the charm of Tim's sneaking admiration for her daring. Tim had lived near the bush long enough to have an immense respect for its dangers and, disregarding the foolish way she had got lost, he now looked at Tamara with a certain envy. She might be a bit silly, but she was brave, too.

'For ages. All night, really. I guess we haven't done that for a long time, not without getting mad at each other and ending up shouting. We're too alike in temperament, Dad says, that's why we tend to fight. We're natural fighters, it helps burn up our excess energy. It's when we hold things in that everything gets twisted and distorted and misunderstood. We're going to talk lots more from now on. Dad says he can see his phone bills going through the roof, but we've gotta keep the lines of communication open, wherever we are.'

'Didn't he want any dinner?' Clare asked tentatively. Hardly any sleep after hours of worry, and then to be tricked into an icy bath! If he was ill, it would be her fault.

'I think Shari was bringing him something. He was still on the phone when I left. Efrem had a cancellation or something, and there's a chance that Dad could go to Russia. If he does, he said I could go too, even if it's term time, 'cause I shouldn't have to wait as long as he did to visit the place where most of my ancestors lived.'

Russia! A whole world away. But then, David was that anyway. Clare could no more prevent herself visiting his room later than she could prevent herself loving him. She had to know that he was really all right.

The excuse seemed a trifle thin when the door opened to her knock and Shari stood there with a tray of dirty dishes. Clare felt herself blush and Shari grinned.

'He's not here.'

'Oh.' Or was he just avoiding her?

'He's been rushed off to hospital with triple-pneumonia.'

It was such a vivid pronouncement of her exaggerated fears that Clare missed the significance of Shari's dancing eyes. *'What?'*

'Hey, Clare, I was only kidding,' said Shari hastily. 'He's fine, he just went off for a swim.'

'A *swim*?'

'A devil for punishment, huh?' Shari's grin re-appeared. Clare had the feeling that she was going to get more ribbing from the episode than ever David would. Talk about the biter bit! 'No, he said he wanted to try out the pool. Actually, he said that parts of him still weren't properly thawed yet.' She waggled her eye-brows suggestively. 'I wonder which parts he was talking about. Want me to keep an eye on Tim for you?'

'He's showing Tamara a new game on the computer,' murmured Clare before pulling herself together. 'Why would I want you to keep an eye on him?'

'No reason,' said Shari innocently, hitching up the tray as she closed the door behind her. 'I just thought you might like a bit of free time...'

Clare was appalled to think she was so transparent. 'Shari——'

'He did say to tell you if you asked where he was, so maybe he's sort of expecting you. That was a pretty rotten thing you did. He *is* a guest, you know...' She trailed off in a giggle. 'If he put the hard word on Miles, who knows, you could get fired for insubordination.'

'David wouldn't be that petty,' said Clare stoutly.

'No, I suppose he is rather a great guy,' Shari agreed. 'Shari!'

'Clare!' Shari imitated her exasperation. 'What I want to know is... what did he do that made you want to cool him off?'

Clare blushed again and Shari laughed. 'You do what you want to do, Clare...I'll keep an eye on Tim *anyway*. And just in case, I'll post an out-of-bounds sign on the track...'

* * *

'What took you so long?'

A few minutes later Clare was staring down at the man drifting lazily towards her across the semi-circular pool which was almost entirely enclosed by the rocky shoreline, spilling out through a narrow channel into the lake proper. The water was wreathed in steam and the moonlight filtered through it to cast a ghostly glow on the pale figure in the water. Was he wearing anything? Clare couldn't see, and from the mocking smile on his face David had detected her flush even in the dark moon-shadows cast by the trees overhanging the track.

There was mockery also in the drawling voice, and Clare toyed with the idea of acting surprised, of pretending she was just out for a stroll. But her towel gave her away.

What am I doing here? she asked herself in momentary panic. If I'm not back in half an hour Shari will *know*... and by osmosis all the rest of them will *know*... Know what? That she was chasing David? So what? He was very chaseable! And very sure of himself, too, by the look of him. Goodness knew why he had manoeuvred her into this situation, but Clare was determined that he was going to get more than he'd bargained for. This morning had given her a taste of freedom... the pleasure of acting unpredictably, on impulse, and to hell with responsibility and common sense. Whatever else she couldn't have... she could have *this*. Clare took a deep breath and began to unbutton her thick, hand-knitted jacket.

'I couldn't decide whether I wanted to come or not,' she said truthfully. 'I thought it might be a trick.'

He was at the side of the pool now, not far from her booted feet, leaning against the side with his chin on steamy folded arms.

'You thought I might be lurking in the bush somewhere, ready to leap out and push you in the lake?' he asked, midnight eyes watching the progress of her fumbling fingers. I'm going to watch you undress for me, was their silent message, and Clare knew that he was deliberately trying to make her feel self-conscious and embarrassed.

'The thought did cross my mind,' she admitted.

'My methods are much more subtle.' The sensuous half-smile confirmed her theory. Clare hoped he couldn't see how her hands shook as she folded the jacket neatly and placed it at a safe distance from the pool. 'You're not going to apologise, are you?' he realised as she ignored his provocation and took off her boots.

'No. It serves you right for being so juvenile. Trying to impress me with your prowess, like a teenager flexing his muscles! Or was it the fact that you can't bear the thought of anyone being better than you at *any*thing?' She began on her blouse.

'You were the one who started it, suggesting I was some puny city boy,' he pointed out, slicking his hair back, spraying cool droplets of water from his arm over her bare feet in the process. 'After I'd come to apologise for what I said yesterday! I was... angry, confused... It shook me, Tamara turning to you instead of me and you accepting her with open arms... and heart. You've never been so generous with *me*.' As if he'd been jealous of both of them.

'You ask a great deal more than Tamara does,' Clare prevaricated, reluctantly unfastening the last button, her courage beginning to waver.

'Mmm.' David's mind wasn't really on the conversation. He was wondering what kind of suit she was wearing. A one-piece, no doubt, as modest as they come. 'Whatever you said to her must have been effective, because she actually deigned to make a deal. Did she tell you?' Clare shook her head. 'She won't go back to the school that suspended her, she'll go to a day school in Auckland and board at the music school. If—*if* she makes an honest attempt to work and sort out her options for next year—and I don't mean she has to get great marks, just a good character, I'm not asking for miracles, after all—then she can come on tour in the holidays, and to Russia, if that comes off. She wasn't ecstatic, but then neither was I, so we've settled for an armed truce... Where in the *hell* is your *suit*?' He jerked upright with the hoarse cry.

'I didn't bring one,' said Clare calmly as she shrugged off her blouse, revealing the camisole beneath. She wasn't wearing a bra, and the cold air instantly made it obvious. She reached for the zip on her slacks.

'You mean you swim here in the nude?' David pushed away from the edge to stand, hands on hips beneath the water which lapped against the thick spread of hair on his chest. He looked quaintly disapproving.

'Not usually.'

'Did you think that was why I asked you out here, to go skinny-dipping?' he demanded, not liking the way the tables had been turned.

Clare pulled off her slacks and imitated his stance. In skimpy lace panties and camisole, it was dramatically effective. 'Didn't you?'

'No, dammit, I didn't,' said David raggedly. 'The joke's gone far enough, Clare. Put on your suit before someone comes.'

'I told you, I didn't bring one. And nobody's going to come.' She toyed nervously with the lace edging at the bottom of the camisole. David's stunned eyes were riveted by the motion.

'How do you know?'

'Because I told them not to.'

'You told——' Black eyes shot with silver moonlight whipped up to hers. His were wary, baffled and...hungry. He swore. 'I didn't get you down here to seduce you, Clare. I just wanted to...to...all right, to pay you back a little. But also to settle unfinished business between us.'

'You mean you *are* wearing something?' Business? Clare didn't want to be serious; she wanted action, not talk!

'Yes! Dammit, Clare, this relationship is not going anywhere until——' His stern command was cut off by a winded sigh. Clare had taken a deep breath and peeled off the camisole. The briefs followed, and for a moment she stood gilded in the moonlight before she gracefully slid into the water. David stood, eyes closed, head thrown back, body stiff with outrage and arousal as Clare moved closer and waited until he opened his eyes again.

Steam had already dewed her face, and the moonlight tracking across the lake into the little pool mocked him with its glimmering caress of the ripe breasts just below the waterline.

'Clare, I don't know what you think you're doing——'

'You don't know? Poor David. Shall I show you?' Her hand briefly rested on the taut muscle bunched at the juncture of neck and shoulder before sliding down under the steamy surface. The hairy roughness then smoothness of his stomach was exciting, but when her fingers skimmed the edge of his trunks there was a churning of the water as he grabbed her wrist in iron fingers.

'OK, Clare, I admit that I thought we might indulge in a little light lovemaking, but we're not giddy teenagers unable to control our desire——'

'Speak for yourself...' Thwarted of her need to touch him with her hands, she stepped closer, her thigh brushing lightly against his, her full breasts nudging his chest. The clenched tension in his body was a seduction in itself. She looked up into his smouldering eyes and smiled. Was that steam or sweat on his brow? She reached up with her other hand to touch and taste. The moisture was salty. She sucked it from her finger, and he groaned and caught that hand too.

'Clare, we agreed to take the time——'

'*You* agreed. You made that decision on your own without consulting me. Well, now I've made mine.'

He misunderstood her. 'Good. Tell me what it is, and then I can stop acting noble. It's crippling me.' In answer to the silky caress of her thigh, his body arched involuntarily into hers, a hiss of agony escaping his clenched teeth.

'Oh, no, no more of your sexual blackmail,' Clare told him ruthlessly. 'I'm not going to be manoeuvred to some private piece of music you have composed in your head. You may make deals with your daughter, but you don't make them with me. I've decided I want you. Here. Now. No procrastinations, no evasions. Just yes or no.' She leaned forward to take a small bite of his smooth, rigid shoulder, lowering her lids to hide the pain of her uncertainty. She had never seduced a man before, let alone an unwilling one, and she was rather shocked at her own boldness. But she loved him so much, she *had* to have him, quickly, before the world crashed in on them again. 'What's it going to be, David?' She licked the small indentations her teeth had made, and suddenly felt herself hauled against him, her hands forced into the small of her back.

'*Yes!* It has to be yes,' he whispered harshly in the steamy stillness. He pressed warningly against her hands, letting her feel the fullness she had teased into life. Released from the rigid restraints he had placed on himself, he was suddenly in full command again, no longer the victim but the victor. He saw the flicker of doubt in her eyes as she realised what she had aroused, and smiled grimly. 'If sex is all you want, I'm happy to oblige. It's a long time since I've had a woman.'

'David——' Was that all she would be, a faceless body?

'But that's not what you want either, is it, Clare? Don't worry, I'll make it good for you. And when we're finished we'll do it again and again until you realise that the act alone will never be enough...'

'David, please...' She wasn't concentrating on his quiet words, but on the way his mouth moved around them, and he saw the possessive hunger in her eyes and knew she required proof.

The sweet wildness was like nothing that Clare had ever known. There were no gentle preliminaries, just a savage consummation of days and nights of sensuous longings. If they had been on a bed, or on the green grass of the bank, Clare knew that her creamy skin would have been bruised, but the water, with its enervating heat and dragging resistance, softened the erotic clash of their bodies to a slow dance of passionate intensity. Only once did David make an effort to restrain the compulsion. Before the first thrust of his possession he hesitated.

'Is it all right?'

'Oh, David...' Her voice was a velvety murmur, lost in the realisation of a dream. 'It's very...*very* all right...'

After it was over, Clare knew that David was right. It *wasn't* enough. Even though she had been shattered by unimagined bliss, she didn't want him to leave her, and cried out at the unbearable sense of loss when he gently withdrew.

'Shhh...sweet girl.' He handled her with exquisite care. 'Come out or we'll drown...or melt...or both...' He helped her out of the pool and dried her body with the thick towel before spreading it on the grass, and lowering her on to it. Clare watched him rescue his trunks from the pool, unable to meet his eyes but fascinated by the undulations of his superbly masculine body. As he turned to join her on the towel, she drew a choked breath. He might be unselfconscious of his own nudity, but he wasn't indifferent to hers.

He lay on his side, not touching her, and waited for her to rediscover her boldness. When her eyes fluttered to his at last, he gave her a slow smile.

'And that was just the rhapsody.' When she blinked, he explained huskily, 'The enthusiastic, extravagant section of my private composition.'

'O...oh?' Clare *was* melting, but it had nothing to do with external skin temperature.

His eyes gleamed. 'You didn't think I only had one string to my bow, did you?' Her eyes flickered down, and he laughed in that same, slow, husky tone that was a symphony in itself. He touched her knee, very lightly, and sketched a leisurely line to her hip, tracing the vulnerable, blue-veined flesh to the pulse point at the very top of her thigh. It leapt against the sensitive tip of his finger. 'We still have the adagio...' he sipped from her parted lips '...the slow movement. And the scherzo...' his hand brushed lightly across the honeyed curls he had dried so lovingly '...so light and playful...the caprices, the variations...not to mention the encores...I never play only one. I don't believe in the old adage about leaving your audience wanting.... Would you like me to run through my whole repertoire, sweet?'

'We can't...' she said breathlessly, wanting it more than she had ever wanted anything in her life.

'That's what I said, but you overruled me, remember? To withhold my favours was sexual blackmail. To be fair, you have to give me the opportunity to acquit myself of such a heinous crime. You must be my judge, my jury, my advocate...'

He acquitted himself very well, Clare had to admit much later. So much later, she didn't dare ask to see the waterproof watch that was David's only apparel. She didn't want to get dressed, she just wanted to lie forever in his arms, rocked to the sweet, sensual music he had created in her heart.

'It's getting late. Our reputations will be well and truly shattered.' David was the first to stir, and Clare resented it.

'What do you care? You're not the one who has to stay and face the...music.' It was a feeble pun which didn't disguise the sting of her first words. Clare hastily began to pull on her clothes. She was supposed to be handling this maturely. She had rehearsed her graceful exit, so why couldn't she stick to it?

Because David wouldn't let her. 'Are you? Staying at Moonlight? Is that what you want?'

She didn't know what he was asking. To block off malicious hope, she said quickly, 'No, actually. I haven't told Miles yet, but I'm going to move to Auckland...with Tim.'

'You're letting him come to the Music School?' David froze in the act of pulling on his sweater. Clare nodded and he slowly completed the task. 'And when did you decide this?'

'I . . . on Saturday night. I . . . I couldn't tell you until I'd talked to Tim,' she added hastily, seeing the menacing tightening of his jaw, 'and Miles . . . I can't just leave him in the lurch. I——'

'But you knew when you followed me down here tonight. You could have put me out of my damned misery straight away, but no, you had to turn it into some sexual farce——'

'*You* were the one who made it such an issue——' she began defensively.

'Because I love you, dammit!' he thundered at her. 'Because it was important that you do it for Tim and for yourself—because it was *right*—not because of *me*, not as a kind of pay-off for my love!' His voice calmed and gentled when he saw her pale, stunned expression, but it was still thick with exasperated temper. 'When you've lost someone, the way you and I have, it's easier to contemplate accepting sex back in your life than *love*. But, believe me, sex is nothing without the emotional responses to back it up. We couldn't have made fantastic love the way we did tonight unless there was more than just biological impulse behind it, Clare. You might have thought, when Lee died, that you would never fall in love again . . . you would never *let* yourself fall in love again, because it hurt too much. I thought that, too, after Nina died. But I was wrong. We both were . . .'

'What are you saying?' Clare whispered helplessly.

'I rather thought I was being extremely explicit,' said David ruefully. 'I love you. I believe you love me. I want to marry you. I want us to build a life together. I want your son to be my son and my daughter to be your daughter. I think we'd make one hell of a family. The future can be *ours*, Clare . . .'

'But . . . what kind of marriage would it be?' she made herself ask, feeling for the ground with feet that suddenly seemed to be hovering hazily above it. 'With you always on tour, and me in Auckland with Tim . . .'

'Only temporarily. As soon as Tim settles in, you'll be free to travel...to live your own life again.'

Don't you mean *yours*? thought Clare hollowly. He assumed too much with his extravagant declaration of love. She wouldn't just be marrying David, she would be marrying *Deverenko*, and she didn't think she was ready for that. To hear him say 'I love you' had been like the answer to a prayer, but it had been a thoughtless prayer. Why, he hadn't even *asked* if she loved him, he had just arrogantly assumed it, just as he assumed that it gave him the right to casually rearrange her life to fit his. How could he love her when he knew so little of her? The kind of freedom he was suggesting would be like a portable prison...trailing around after her famous husband, clinging to the fringes of his busy life, doomed to constant comparison with his vivacious and equally famous first wife. She would not only be utterly dependent on David financially and emotionally, but socially, too, living a life of empty, unfulfilling glamour. She would need to flex her wings before she could even hope to swoop to the heights that David soared at with any confidence.

'David...I don't really know *what* my own life is yet... I need some time. It's too soon...' She swallowed, wishing the moonlight didn't show his face quite so clearly. She wasn't sure whether it was truly his heart or his pride that she was hurting, but he was definitely stricken by her rejection. But he had rejected *her*, saying that she needed time. Surely he would understand if she asked for more? 'I...I don't know if I'm cut out to be the kind of wife you want. I...I mean, I'm flattered that you should ask, but I don't think I'm ready for anything so permament just yet...' Oh, that had come out all horribly wrong! David stiffened.

'You want something *im*permanent? You want an *affair*? A string of one-night stands? For that's what an affair would amount to!'

He made it sound sordid and cheap, and yet the thought that she might not have to give him up completely blinded her for a moment. 'It's better than rushing into a marriage that we might regret...'

'So!' He had never looked, nor sounded, so foreign, everything about him thunderously dark. 'I offer you my name, my honour, my lifelong love and respect, and you offer me occasional *sex*!' He spat the word like a curse. 'Why? *Why?* Why do you run from love? If I give you time, how will you use it? To intellectualise away your feelings? To dig yourself back into a boring, placid existence where nothing can challenge your smug, emotional complacency?'

'That's not fair!'

'Fair? Is it fair that you should make me love you, and then callously trample my heart into the mud?'

'Is it fair that you suddenly fling marriage in my face and demand an instant answer? Should I have grovelled in gratitude because you want me to become a member of your entourage——?'

'I don't have an entourage——' he interrupted with words that were tongues of fire sheathed in ice.

'Well, I have other plans. I'm damned good at what I do, and it so happens that there's a job opening up in Auckland that would just suit the kind of training I've had, *and* enable me to be on hand if Tim needs me.' She took a deep breath, knowing it was a bad time to tell him, while they were throwing insults at each other, but he would have to know some time. 'Brenda told me that the Music School is going to need a new House Mother soon. I've already applied.'

The last bitter words in the argument were howled to the moon in furious denial: *'Over my dead body!'*

CHAPTER TEN

CLARE rose to her feet to join in the thunderous ovation for the artists on the platform. Inside, her emotions were equally tumultuous. David had played with his customary brilliance, but it was his appearance which had riveted her. He looked as haggard as she felt. What was the matter with him? And why had he brought *that woman* with him? She hadn't been scheduled to appear with him on his short tour of New Zealand. Clare glared at her. Anna Federov was every bit as gorgeous as Tamara had claimed.

For months Clare had been haunted by the wretched woman, and now she was expected to applaud her! Clare's hands fell limply to her sides.

When David had left Moonlight, after failing to bully, cajole, wheedle, blackmail or seduce Clare into seeing things his way, Tamara had accompanied him with a parting shot that had been devastatingly to the mark. The girl had felt bitterly betrayed over the abortive proposal, which her father had made no effort to keep secret. Even though Clare had refused him, Tamara evidently intended to make sure she never changed her mind.

'Dad just decided it was time I needed a mother, that's why he asked you to marry him. Stuck down here where you don't have any competition, he might have fooled himself into thinking he's in love with you, but wait until he gets to the States and sees Anna Federov again! She's going to be his accompanist, you know. She's a brilliant pianist and she's spectacularly beautiful, and Dad's always admired her. She's part Russian, too. They have simply *everything* in common.' Tamara tossed her head, hurt and intent on hurting. 'They'll be working together and living at the same hotels and attending the same parties… If anyone has a chance of replacing my mother, Anna has. Dad won't even give *you* a second thought!'

And nor, judging by his actions since, had he.

Beside her, Tim had scrambled up on to his seat to applaud, almost bursting with awe and pride. In the six months he had been at the Deverenko Music School his shy, solitary nature had blossomed. No longer did he prefer the company of his violin and his books to that of other children. He had become best friends with his room-mate and had even spent a few weekends at Christopher's home. He hadn't had an asthma attack or nightmare in months.

Clare's elbow was jogged and she smiled quickly at the girl on the other side of her. Tamara was still inclined to be moody and unpredictable, but she had changed almost as much as Tim. True to her promise to her father, she was gritting her teeth and making the best of things. She enjoyed her status as a special boarder at the Music School, and even rose earlier than necessary in the morning to join in the exercise session. She laughed more than she pouted, and no longer hid behind that offputting mock-sophistication. She had even conspicuously put aside her animosity to Clare, and now acted as if she had almost forgotten about the rocky start to their relationship.

For Clare had got the job that she had sought at the Deverenko Music School—possibly because she had the inside knowledge to apply even before the position was advertised. Her experience at Moonlight and Miles's fulsome reference had clinched the application, once she had reassured the principal that she had no intention of 'interfering' with Tim's education or discipline. Clare was now responsible for the health and welfare of thirteen girls, aged nine to fifteen, including Tamara. It was an interesting job, fun, and at times exhausting. It was a little more—and a lot less—than she had expected it to be. It kept her busy and catapulted her into quite an active social life involving the other staff, the children and their parents, and the wider cultural connections the school sustained. Virginia, who had mellowed now that Tim was getting everything she had wanted for him, was delighted that Clare had come out of her 'self-imposed exile'. Clare looked at her now, beaming at the stage, delighted by her tenuous connection with the maestro. Thank heavens she had never learned that David had asked Clare to marry him. To be Deverenko's *mother-in-law*...even one marriage removed!

Clare shifted restlessly. Everything was going swimmingly, so why was she the only one fighting against the current? She wasn't happy, and she had known it for some time, but she wasn't quite sure what to do about it. The reason was simple; she was more in love with David than ever. Life without him was every bit as empty and unfulfilling as she had been afraid that life *with* him would have been. Only, Deverenko didn't seem to care. He had been back to the school several times in the past few months to conduct classes, but not once had he treated Clare with anything but polite respect. He hadn't mentioned love, let alone marriage. He had been friendly but, worse than that, he had been *kind*. He had even taken Clare out to dinner a couple of times, and once on a picnic with Tamara and Tim, but there had been no hint of passion, even when she had discreetly indicated it would be welcome.

She could have made the first move herself but, having dealt such a crushing blow to his pride, she thought that he had earned the right to take the lead. She must accept and follow but—oh, it was *agony*. Every time he left he took a little bit more of her heart and happiness with him. Dammit, she was the one who had sent him away, and yet *she* was the one who now felt betrayed!

Feeling as she did, she would have loved to escape the post-concert gathering, but of course she couldn't. David hugged his daughter exuberantly, with a laughing caution about his latest phone bill. He shook hands happily with Tim, and greeted Virginia with a warm kiss on the cheek. Clare received a cool nod which she returned. Her only defence was to retain her dignity and reflect his own indifference.

Unfortunately Anna was with him, hanging possessively on his arm. Tamara had spent the night at her father's house, after his flight arrived late the previous night. Had Anna stayed there, too? Clare could hardly bear to be introduced. She felt sick with bitter, black jealousy, totally alien to her experience. She smiled, but violet-grey storm-clouds boiled across her eyes as she saw the woman was even more beautiful at close range. How could mortal man resist her, even if he wanted to?

She tore her eyes away and found herself looking deep into David's fathomless black gaze. Arrogant, faithless swine! She stared at him defiantly, not hiding her contempt, and to her shock he suddenly smiled—a wolfish, sensual grin that turned her inside-out. He knew how she felt, and he was laughing at her! At that moment she hated him more than she had ever loved him.

Anna was asking Tamara about her interests, and Clare forced herself to ignore David and listen. For one who had once described her in such glowing terms, Tamara seemed strangely indifferent to the woman's charm, edging away from her towards Clare, and mentioning the local gym they had both joined a few months ago. Tamara was thoroughly hooked on fitness, and even talking about a career as an aerobics instructor. She was still thin, but she was beginning to fill out and develop a muscular sleekness that was very attractive. The school's healthy diet and plenty of exercise had done wonders for her skin, and her hair was a shiny, bouncy bob.

'And what about music?' Anna was pressing insistently, trying hard to establish a dialogue with the reluctant girl.

Tamara shrugged again, one eye on her father. 'I play the piano at school.'

'Tamara?' David looked at her with wary delight.

Tamara pinkened at the effect of her surprise. She had been in two minds about it, badgering Clare to reassure

her that David wouldn't make 'too big a thing' of it.
'We have jam sessions some nights and everyone does
something. I was pretty rusty, so I signed up for some
lessons at school. Actually, I like playing the synthesiser
better,' she said, to assert herself. 'It's more versatile
than the piano.'

Anna raised her eyebrows at David, as if expecting
him to protest the offence to classical tradition, but he
merely grinned in reply. The grin highlighted the new
leanness to his face, and Clare studied him hungrily. It
was more than just tiredness, there was an edge to
David's exhaustion, a rawness that was new. As if he
had reached the end of his tether, as if he no longer had
the strength to rein in all the violent energy that sustained his artistic and personal drive. She felt suddenly
afraid for him, and her concern burst out, in a voice
that was slightly too sharp for politeness, 'Have you been
ill? You look terrible.'

David's musician's ear detected the pitched tension.
He turned his head slowly and looked at her. 'It's been
a long six months,' he said, and she forgot to breathe.
Those polite, empty black eyes were suddenly speaking
to her again, and she was afraid to try and understand
what they said. 'Particularly this last tour. Six European
cities in ten days, a prisoner of hotel-rooms and concert
halls...it's pretty gruelling. Perhaps I'm getting too old
for it all...'

'Don't be absurd, David,' Anna laughed in her husky
brown voice. 'You love it! And you did have a break...
Remember when we were snowed in for two days in
Berlin? You certainly weren't complaining about your
age *then*!' Clare could have murdered her then and there
for her revolting coyness. 'You're at your peak, David.'

'He won't stay there long if his health breaks down,'
said Clare thinly.

'David needs to play as he needs to breathe, and if he
must suffer a little in the process...' an eloquent shrug
that emphasised her lovely bare shoulders above a
beautiful black gown '...all great artists suffer for their

art. The European critics say he is better than ever. "A new fire in his interpretation that richly complements a superhuman technique,"' she quoted, as if that put an end to the matter.

'And that's all you care about, his playing?' demanded Clare hotly, appalled by the callous attitude. 'What about his *life*? What use is a dead musical genius?'

Someone gasped at her bluntness, and Anna smiled pityingly. 'David's genius is immortal. He's made recordings that will give pleasure to millions for generations to come.'

'And do any of those millions give a damn for David as a human being? Do you? Would you stick around if he got sick and couldn't play any more? Or would you just whip out some of his recordings and substitute the music for the man? I think all that about suffering artists is a load of rubbish! It's just an excuse for people to ease their own consciences, so *they* don't have to suffer!'

Anna's dark eyes flashed, her long black hair swirling like silk over her shoulders. 'You have no conception of what you are talking. What are you? Some sort of domestic employee at David's school who happens to have a talented child? I suggest you——'

'Ladies...ladies...' David intervened at last, with the lazy satisfaction of a sultan breaking up a fight among his concubines. Clare, humiliated that she had betrayed herself, took a vicious swipe at his conceit.

'You may still play like an angel, David, but you look a wreck,' she told him bluntly. 'I think you should see a doctor. Do they starve you on these tours? You look as if you've lost a lot of muscle tone.'

Anna wasn't going to be silenced, either. 'Of course we don't starve. David's manager always organises first-class accommodation.'

'You mean his secretary does, from his office in New York.' Clare knew from Tamara that Efrem conducted most of his business with David by phone, unless David was appearing on the American East Coast. 'And since his manager takes a percentage cut of David's income, it's in his interests to keep him in constant work. Who looks after David's personal requirements? Makes sure he doesn't forget to eat and sleep like the rest of us more ordinary mortals? *You?*' Clare raised her eyebrows in magnificent scepticism. 'If so, you're not doing a very good job.'

'David is a mature man, quite capable of looking after himself; he doesn't need a nursemaid!' snapped Anna, on the defensive as everyone looked at the unmistakable signs of exhaustion on David's face, the taut skin by his shadowed eyes, the febrile flush that lay along his cheekbones as he endured the inspection. 'He's had a slight case of flu, that's all...we both did. In fact, I was the one who caught it first, just before Berlin.' Her smile cut Clare to the heart. 'Perhaps I passed on the infection...'

'Let's hope that's the only infection you passed on,' Clare muttered but, to her horror, there was a lapse in conversation in the crowd around them and her words were clearly audible.

There was a moment of shrieking silence. Clare went scarlet with embarrassment. She closed her eyes, hoping she could shrink into a small, dark hole in the floor.

A hand closed possessively on her wrist. 'Excuse us, won't you?' she heard David say through her cringing haze. 'I believe Clare wants to apologise for that appalling lapse in manners in private. She's shy like that. Virginia, will you see to Tamara and Tim?'

Clare was dragged through the gathering like a prisoner in a chain gang. This was the second time she had made a scene in public over David, and it was all his fault!

'I'm not going to apologise,' she hissed furiously as she stumbled along an empty corridor after him. 'She was asking for it. She was practically raping you with her eyes!'

'It's just her way,' dismissed David as he tried first one side door and then another, and muttered something in Russian when he found them locked.

'Oh, I see,' gritted Clare. 'How nice for you. No wonder you're looking so gaunt and exhausted. You must have trouble keeping up with her. She must be young enough to be your daughter!'

'Not quite.' He tried another door and rattled it impatiently when it too was locked.

He wasn't denying it! Clare dug the nails of her free hand into the back of his hand.

'Ouch!' His grip didn't budge. 'Don't damage my hands, Clare.'

'Why? Are you afraid Anna might dump you if you can't play any more?'

'I'm sure she would.' Her mouth fell open at his uncaring shrug. 'Look, Clare, despite the open invitation, I haven't slept with Anna and I don't intend to.'

'But...she...you...' She faltered under the power of his dark stare, and then rallied. 'You let everyone think....'

'It was the only thing that seemed to get a rise out of you.' His mouth curved, his dark eyes gleaming. 'You hated her the moment you laid eyes on her, didn't you? If looks could kill, Anna would have been dead on the platform.'

'I...no...' Clare could feel herself weakening, melting as she always seemed to do when he looked at her, touched her, whether in passion or in anger.

'Ah, Clare, that's the first spark of life I've seen in you for months...'

'You haven't *seen* me for months.'

'Not through *my* choice. That was your idea, that we could live perfectly well without each other. I have bookings that run five *years* into the future, commitments that I am morally obliged to fulfil. I *had* to leave. But I don't have to like it. You're to blame for the way I look, Clare. It's not too much sex that's draining me, it's too little love.'

Clare thought she would faint. She stared at him dizzily, her head buzzing. He jerked on her hand and she stumbled against him, and for a moment she dreamed he was going to kiss her, but then there was a noise at the other end of the hallway and he turned to the nearest door. It resisted his temper. 'Dammit, is there nowhere private in this whole bloody building?' he howled in majestic frustration.

'You looking for the piano, Mr Deverenko?'

An elderly man, wearing an impressively hand-knitted cardigan, was shuffling down the hall towards them.

David raised a wordless eyebrow while Clare tried to hide her still manacled wrist in the side-folds of her slinky silk dress.

'That's the piano-room,' said the old man, tipping them both a grin. 'Where we store the Steinway. But we haven't brought it down yet. It's still on the platform.'

'You mean the room is empty?'

'Yep.'

'But it's locked.'

'Rules. I gotta key here.' He produced it and they all looked at it in silence. The old man's rheumy eyes twinkled when they met David's covetous look. 'Won't be bringing down the piano till after your last concert tomorrow, but I guess there isn't any sense in locking an empty room.'

'I guess there isn't,' said David, and watched him unlock it and re-pocket the key.

'Thanks. We'll be sure to leave everything the way we find it,' David told him, and the old man chuckled.

'Ain't anything there to muss up. Have a nice evening, sir, miss...'

Clare's cheeks were hot as David slid back the wide door and pulled her into the darkness of a windowless room. He felt along the wall and switched on the light. The room was bare, save for a heap of dustsheets untidily folded on the bare polished floor.

'You know what he thought...'

'He thought that we were sneaking away to make mad, passionate love on the sly.' David let her go at last and she rubbed her lightly throbbing wrist. 'Was he so far wrong?'

'I...yes!' Clare put an uneasy few steps between them, eyeing him warily. She didn't know him in this reckless mood.

'You mean, if I slid that tiny strap off your shoulder and put my mouth against that luscious cream-and-freckle breast of yours, you won't sigh and press against me and shiver with sinful delight?'

'D-David!' As if the words were the deed, Clare shielded herself from his hot gaze, feeling her nipples bud betrayingly against her palms. The dress was a simple slip of silk, flaring from the low waist, requiring a bare minimum of underwear.

'Are you denying it?' His voice thickened and hardened. 'You want me, Clare. I only have to touch you and I feel the heat under your skin, the passion, the need. You were jealous out there. You couldn't bear the idea of my touching another woman the way I touched you. Doesn't that tell you something? Haven't you learned *anything* this last six months? You know, you never told me that you loved me, you never had the courage. But you didn't have to say the words then and you don't have to say them now. I *know*...I can taste it, feel it, scent it...' Her hands clutched to her breasts, Clare was rooted to the spot as he prowled closer, his silky truths binding her to him, his dark eyes penetrating to her soul, baring its secrets. 'Six months ago, you made a choice. Are you regretting it? *Are* you, Clare?' Plea, threat, promise—the question held them all.

'No.' The fire in his eyes died, to be instantly revived. 'It was right for me...*then*. I'm a naturally cautious person and nothing can change that, David. I like to be sure about things. I *needed* this time to come to terms with what loving you meant.' He touched her, very lightly, and she trembled with the knowledge of love.

'I...I've loved working at the school...the girls are darlings,' wryly, 'even Tamara. But, after the responsibilities of running Moonlight more or less on my own, it's really not stretching me as I thought it would. I mean, it's not something I want to make a career out of. What was right for me six months ago isn't right for me now.'

'And what *is* right for you now?'

'You.'

'You're sure?' He was taking it step by step. This time there were to be no mistakes.

Clare nodded, her grey eyes clear. 'Very sure. I love you. I . . . I want to marry you.' She blushed, and he laughed and swept her into his arms at last.

'Is this a proposal?'

'Very definitely a proposal!'

'I accept!' And he did so, with enthusiasm.

When she could breathe again, Clare said 'I missed you. You were so polite. So horribly *nice*.'

'It was either that or beat you, and you had proved rather immune to the macho approach.' His grin faded as he stilled her against him. 'But underneath my anger, I think I knew that you were right not to let me sweep you off your feet, as if we were teenagers responsible only for ourselves. I'm too used to getting my own way; I took it for granted that I would continue to do so. I had no right to do that. As penance I made myself stand back, and let you say your farewells to the past. That's what the waiting was all about wasn't it? Farewell, and hail the new beginning?' With a shock of insight she realised he was right. 'You got that job at the school so easily, Clare, because I recommended you for it,' he said quietly. 'Oh, not just because you wanted it, or because I wanted to keep tabs on you and Tim,' he added quickly when she flinched, 'but because I knew that you would do the job well, regardless of any personal motives you might have. I'd seen you with Tamara. Although she wasn't your child, and she behaved abominably towards you much of the time, you still treated her with respect, and were thoughtful of her needs. You're a gentle person, Clare, but you stand by the things you believe in and that makes you strong. I couldn't imagine anyone better to look after my child when she is away from me. From reports, I gather there are other parents who feel the same. I'll be resented for taking away one of the best House Mothers we've had.'

'You're not *taking*,' said Clare huskily. 'I'm giving.'

'Oh, but I am. I want more than just a lover and wife, you see. I was hoping that the last six months might have made you more comfortable in the musical milieu, less of an outsider...'

'Well, yes, I suppose I am... a bit.' She was puzzled by his diffidence, the hint of excitement.

'Because you put your finger on it back there, when you were wiping the floor with my beautiful accompanist. Efrem is a wunderkind at wheeling and dealing, and a great friend, but he spends most of his time in New York. He has a business to run and other temperamental musicians to look after. I need someone on the spot—to see off the inevitable sharks, to help humanise my itineraries, to make my appointments and help write my speeches, to protect me from overwork and defend me against the Press, to host parties for me—in short, to make my life liveable again. Does that sound challenging enough, do you think?'

'Oh, David, you don't have to *bribe* me to marry you,' Clare cried, trying to hide her secret delight.

'It's no sinecure, Clare,' he warned wryly. 'I'm not creating the job simply to give you something to do. If you don't want to take it on, that's fine, but sooner or later I'll have to employ a personal assistant. I'm an artist, for pity's sake, I shouldn't have to lower myself to such sweated labour!'

It was such a perfect imitation of Anna's contempt that Clare laughed. 'I suppose I could do it on a trial basis...'

'The job, yes. The marriage, no. I have another week of engagements in New Zealand and then a fortnight of recording in Chicago. Will you come with me? Or would you rather wait?'

This was said with such loaded patience that Clare couldn't resist. 'Well...'

He sighed. 'I suppose we've waited this long . . . a little longer won't kill me.' His eyes slitted as he murmured provocatively, 'At least the critics will approve; while I burn for you, so does my music. *New fire*, they call it...'

Anna's quoted words.

'You're not leaving this country without a ring on your finger.' Clare slid her arms around his neck and moved enticingly within his hard embrace, feeling the heat of him through his formal attire. 'On the other hand,' she teased, 'perhaps we ought to make this a platonic marriage . . . for the sake of your *art*.'

'The hell we will,' he growled against her satiny throat, one hand plunging into the pale gold of her hair while the other discovered the thinness of her dress. He stroked the shape of her, his fingers sliding against the silk, the silk sliding against her skin, exciting them both. 'When I looked over tonight and saw you glaring daggers at me, it was like a cage door being thrown open. After being so careful all this time not to put pressure on you . . . I nearly exploded with joy. Love me, Clare *de lune*, love me the way you did at Moonlight . . .'

'I do, David, I do.'

He groaned, bunching the thin stuff of her dress in his fist, pulling it so that every dip and hollow of her body was outlined to his longing gaze. His smile was crooked. 'That wasn't quite what I meant, although it's nice to know. But you're right, we can't celebrate our love on bare boards and dust sheets. Now, if the *Steinway* was here . . .' He took wicked pleasure in her blush, but she was equal to the challenge.

'I'm sure you'll make love in *grand* style, even without it.'

'Only with you, darling, only with you.' He cupped her face gently. 'Never doubt me. You may doubt that you're special to me, but I *never* have. I love you for just being you, shy and serious, fierce and bold. We'll make lovely music together, Clare.' He kissed away the last of her silly fears, tenderly, as if he knew each and every one of them. 'And perhaps one day we can create something even more precious out of our love. A child that is uniquely *us*.'

Clare stiffened. She had already faced the death of that dream, sweetly regretted but put to rest where dreams belonged. Then she realised—he had said child, not baby.

'You mean...adopt?'

The flicker of shock was smothered by compassion in the dark, velvety gaze. 'You can't have any more children? Oh, Clare, you little idiot, why didn't you tell me? It doesn't make any difference! Is that what you thought? Is that why you took so long to——'

'Not me, *you*. Tamara told me at Moonlight about your...your vasectomy.'

'My *what*?' David dropped her like a hot coal.

'Your vasectomy,' Clare faltered. 'She told me that you'd agreed to be sterilised because her mother had been warned not to get pregnant again.'

'Yes, she was told not to risk another baby, but it was *her* decision to be sterilised, not mine! She wouldn't even consider allowing me to do it. She said no one should be asked to make a sacrifice like that for someone else, even for love. Wait until I get my hands on that wretched girl! And *you*...you thought I would do this, marry you, without bothering to tell you something so vitally affecting your life?' His outrage swung on to Clare, but she was just realising the ramifications of the lie.

'You mean...I could have got *pregnant*?' She looked at him accusingly. 'I...I thought it was safe!'

'So did I,' he confessed ruefully, and at her frown, 'I *did* ask you if it was all right...'

'Yes, but I thought you meant, was I *enjoying* it?' said Clare faintly, as she recalled the circumstances in which his question was asked.

'I think that was fairly obvious,' he teased, and laughed when she buried her hot face in his quaking chest. 'It was mutual, darling. It would have served Tamara right if you *had* got pregnant and Miles had

rounded me up with a shotgun. I shall have a few words
with my lying daughter——'

'No, don't. She said it in the heat of the moment, and
probably forgot all about it. We're friends now. Let's
let sleeping dogs lie.'

'Sleeping dogs? Tamara is very much awake,' said
David as he reluctantly ushered Clare out of the temptation of the empty room, 'and busy working the angles.
She knows that I want you in my life and she's figured
out that I view touring *"en famille"* far more liberally
that I do a teenage girl on her own. It's also a lot more
flexible and enjoyable than dragging around some
strange tutor or chaperon you might or might not like.
Tamara, when she puts her mind to it, can be every bit
as practical as your Tim.'

'Tim?'

'Henderson showed me his latest mathematics brain-
storm. It appears your son has decided that we can't be
relied on to organise ourselves into marriage so he's done
it for us. He drew up a very complicated timetable in-
corporating my published schedule with yours, his and
Tamara's, and put it all through the school's computer
as a maths project. Just to make it more difficult, he
included future projections to allow for family increase,
Juilliard study for him, Tamara's "jazzercising" her way
into her own studio, and—I sense a slight criticism here—
the possibility of me requiring more free time for composition. The spread sheets are flawless...our whole lives
mapped out, complicated as hell but clear as crystal.
Somehow I don't think that anyone on the staff is going
to be the least surprised by any announcement we make.'

'Oh, David!' Clare didn't know whether to be proud
or embarrassed. No wonder she had been getting
sideways grins lately!

'Mmm, and that wasn't the best of it.'

'No?' She loved that soft, musical amusement.

'No.' Her Russian bear bristled with mischief. 'The marks were prophetic, too: A for achievement, A for effort and, of course...' his voice was a husky, gloating growl of triumph, 'A for accuracy!'

2 NEW TITLES
FOR JANUARY 1990

Mariah *by Sandra Canfield is the first novel in a sensational quartet of sisters in search of love…* Mariah's sensual and provocative behaviour contrasts enigmatically with her innocent and naive appearance… Only the maverick preacher can recognise her true character and show her the way to independence and true love.

£2.99

Faye is determined to make a success of the farm she has inherited – but she hadn't accounted for the bitter battle with neighbour, Seth Carradine, who was after the land himself. In desperation she turns to him for help, and an interesting bargain is struck.

Kentucky Woman by Casey Douglas, best selling author of Seasons of Enchantment. **£2.99**

W●RLDWIDE

TASTY FOOD COMPETITION!

How would you like a years supply of Mills & Boon Romances ABSOLUTELY FREE? Well, you can win them! All you have to do is complete the word puzzle below and send it in to us by March. 31st. 1990. The first 5 correct entries picked out of the bag after that date will win **a years supply of Mills & Boon Romances** (*ten books every month - worth £162*) What could be easier?

```
H O L L A N D A I S E R
E Y E G G O W H A O H A
R S E E C L A I R U C T
B T K K A E T S I F I A
E E T I S M A L C F U T
U R C M T L H E E L Q O
G S I U T F O N O E D U
N H L S O T O N E F M I
I S R S O M A C W A A L
R I A E E T I R J A E L
E F G L L P T O T V R E
M O U S S E E O D O C P
```

CLAM	HOLLANDAISE	OYSTERS	SPICE
COD	JAM	PRAWN	STEAK
CREAM	LEEK	QUICHE	TART
ECLAIR	LEMON	RATATOUILLE	
EGG	MELON	RICE	
FISH	MERINGUE	RISOTTO	
GARLIC	MOUSSE	SALT	
HERB	MUSSELS	SOUFFLE	

PLEASE TURN OVER FOR DETAILS ON HOW TO ENTER

HOW TO ENTER

All the words listed overleaf, below the word puzzle, are hidden in the grid. You can find them by reading the letters forward, backwards, up or down, or diagonally. When you find a word, circle it or put a line through it, the remaining letters (which you can read from left to right, from the top of the puzzle through to the bottom) will ask a romantic question.

After you have filled in all the words, don't forget to fill in your name and address in the space provided and pop this page in an envelope (you don't need a stamp) and post it today. Hurry - competition ends March 31st 1990.

Mills & Boon Competition,
FREEPOST,
P.O. Box 236,
Croydon,
Surrey. CR9 9EL

Only one entry per household

Hidden Question _____

_____

Name _____

Address _____

_____

_____

_____ Postcode _____

COMP 8